TUMULTUOUS
too

I0666006

Y.R. PERRY

Copyright © 2019 by Y.R. Perry

All rights reserved. This book or any portion thereof may not be
reproduced or used in any manner whatsoever without the express
written permission of the publisher except for the use of brief quotations
in a book review.

Printed in the United States of America

ISBN: 978-0-578-56256-8

First Printing, 2019

For information, write:

yperry92@gmail.com

Dedication

To women of all walks of life, walking into their worth.
No matter how long it takes or how long it took for you to
discover your value, keep your head up, queen,
so that your crown will never fall again.
The straw that was meant to break you, didn't.
It helped build you!

Tumultuous Too picks up where *Tumultuous* left our readers wondering and hanging like a thread, patiently waiting to see if Yvette had finally found love everlasting. Will this man be everything she ever longed for after so many failed relationships and a marriage? Soul ties, sexual escapades, and heartbreak. Full of lust, blind desires, and lies. Will It be all behind her? Has she finally found the one?

These two books will be summed up in the third sequel, the finale, *Tumultuous Apogee*.

Acknowledgments

Editor: Marvin D. Cloud

Cover Design: Keith Crear of Grizzly Media

Back photo cred: Touche' Harvey of Touche' Studios

Table of Contents

Chapter 1   A Familiar Voice From Hell   1

Chapter 2   Becoming Mrs. Jennings   11

Chapter 3   In the Beginning   15

Chapter 4   Red Flags   21

Chapter 5   Girls Will be Girls   31

Chapter 6   A Wolf in Sheep's Clothing   37

Chapter 7   Mask Off   45

Chapter 8   Joseph Who?   55

Chapter 9   Trying to Control the Uncontrollable   65

Chapter 10   Stranger Danger   77

Chapter 11   Fight or Flight—The Beginning of the End   87

Chapter 12   When the Smoke Clears   103

CHAPTER 1
A FAMILIAR VOICE FROM HELL

The couple stood at the altar in front of friends and families, coworkers, and friends of friends. Everyone dressed in their best, and wore smiles of happiness because Yvette had finally snagged herself a good one. He was handsome, well-spoken, established, and God-fearing. Just what the doctor ordered. The day was beautiful. The venue was incredible. Her bridesmaids and his groomsmen looked amazing. Yvette stood there in her Vera Wang wedding dress. It was ivory in color; a halter top style with beautiful jewel pearls covered the top portion of the dress. The bottom portion was lined, floor-length with a cathedral-styled train, flowered and embroidered. The dress draped down the venue's grass for what seemed like miles when she walked down the aisle to take her place alongside her husband in front of the pastor. "Is there anyone with just cause why these two should not be joined today in holy matrimony, let him on her speak now or forever hold their peace," the minister stated.

"I love you, Yvette! Please don't do this!"

Yvette heard a voice say those words from a distance. She looked around to see where the voice was coming from. *How could he* she thought. She continued to look around to try and find out where the voice was coming from. Everyone else looked around as well. For the life of her, she could not figure out the direction, but she knew it sounded familiar.

1

"Yvette! Yvette," Kelsey whispered and tried to get her attention. Yvette was focused on finding out the source of the voice that she totally ignored her sister. She could hear him but she couldn't see him. "Yvette!" Kelsey said once more. Yvette finally looked at her. "Girl, what's wrong with you? Who are you looking for?"

It was just her imagination. No one was there to disrupt the wedding. No one called out to her. The voice was only in her head. Perhaps it was a telepathic message because it sounded real and clear. Everyone else looked around because they wondered what she was looking at. Yvette stood there in dismay and embarrassment.

"Bitch, snap out of it. What the fuck is wrong with you?" Elisha came in close and whispered in Yvette's ear. Then she politely walked back to her position with the other bridesmaids and smiled nervously at the guests who waited for the ceremony to proceed.

"Babe, what's wrong?" Joseph asked with a look of concern as he held her hands. Yvette held her head down with embarrassment.

She finally looked up at him with tears in her eyes and said, "I'm so sorry, Joseph. I thought I heard someone or something."

"It's okay, babe. Are you all right now?"

"Yes," Yvette replied. "Joseph, I'm so sorry," she repeated once more.

"Babe, I said it's okay. Pastor, you can proceed. We are fine," Joseph directed the minister. He turned to smile at Yvette.

"No," she said. "I don't think you understand, Joseph. I'm sorry. I can't do this."

"What?" Joseph asked in disbelief.

Yvette didn't stick around for the backlash. She quickly bustled her dress, turned away, and ran across the venue's lawn. She dropped the train of her dress as she ran. It dragged across the yard. Lace and embroidered flowers, pearls and rhinestones, glistened in the sun as the grass and uneven ground created patterns in the train of her dress like an ocean full of waves. Her bridesmaids, his groomsmen, guests, and what was supposed to be her future husband, was in disbelief. Once Kelsey recovered from the shock that Yvette had run away and left her future husband at the altar, she took off after her.

Shortly after she moved, Elisha followed, and mumbled along the way. "Oh, no this bitch didn't! I didn't pay my car note to have money to pay for this dress and I took a day off for work with no PTO. She is getting married today!"

In a haze, she took off her shoes and chased after the two. Once inside the venue, Yvette made a beeline to the restroom.

"Stop running, Yvette!" Kelsey yelled. "I'm about to break my ankle in these shoes!"

"Bitch, you should have took them off like I did," Elisha said as she ran past Kelsey. "Who tries to run in stilettos but a crazy person?"

"Yvette did."

"Exactly, a crazy person, as I said."

Inside the restroom, the chase came to a halt. The three panted. They were all out of breath.

"What's going on, Yvette? Why did you leave like that? I thought this was what you wanted. You have a great man, he's God-fearing, he loves you, and he treats you with all the respect in the world. What's wrong?" Kelsey asked with kindness in her eyes.

"Seriously, you guys. I could have sworn I heard a voice calling out to me from somewhere," Yvette responded. "It sounded so clear and real."

"Who the fuck gonna be calling out to you on your wedding day?" Elisha said with anger. "You know a bitch broke. I was barely able to afford this damn dress and excuse me if I'm being insensitive now, but look, there was nobody calling your name out there. Or did you want someone to?

You left a man at the altar and a yard full of guests, waiting. What are you gonna do?"

"Don't push her, Elisha!" Kelsey yelled. "This is a commitment, not to mention a second marriage. Yvette, if you are having cold feet, let's talk it through. The voice you heard or thought you heard, was it a man's voice or a woman's voice? Who did it sound like?"

"It was a man's voice," Yvette said. "It sounded like it could be either Dalvin or Geo."

"Bitch, if you don't gather up that mutha fuckin' dress train, and your mind, and get to that damn altar!"

"Elisha!" Kelsey shouted.

"Girl, trust me. Neither one of their asses will come a-calling at nobody's damn wedding. It's all in your mind," Elisha said. "You better shake that shit off. You have a good man out there, something that all of us women are looking for."

There was a knock at the door.

"Who's there?" Kelsey asked.

"It's Joseph. Yvette, baby, what's wrong?"

"Losing her natural mind," Elisha retorted.

"Be quiet, Elisha," Kelsey warned.

"Baby, please don't do this. I love you. I wanna spend the rest of my life with you."

"Before you answer him, do you love him? I mean really love him?" Kelsey asked. She looked at Yvette with sincerity.

"Yes," she replied. "I do love him."

"What's the problem, bitch? I mean really though?" Elisha asked as she tried to brush her hair back into place after it became disheveled in the chase. "You finally got yourself a king so now you gonna shuffle the deck for those joker ass voices in your head. I promise you neither one of them have you on their radar at all right now."

"Yvette, babe, please open the door. Please?" Joseph pleaded from the other side.

"What are you gonna do, Yvette?" Kelsey asked.

"Everyone is waiting. You have spent all this money. Everyone is dressed and waiting."

"Yeah, what you gone do, bitch?" Elisha questioned. She stared Yvette down. Yvette thought about it for a minute. *He has treated me better than any man that I have dated thus far. He's established, God-fearing, good-looking, and most of all, he loves me. There aren't many good men left out there.*

"Yvette, what are you gonna do, girl?" Kelsey asked with a sense of urgency.

"Tell Joseph I will be out in a minute. Give me a few minutes to get myself together. Find the make up artist. She was supposed to stay for touch ups for the reception photos."

"She should still be around somewhere because you most definitely need some adjustments and a touch up to your beat." They opened the door and went to find the make up artist. Joseph still waited by the door. Kelsey was startled. "Oh, my God, you scared me," she said as she opened the door to see Joseph towering over her.

"What's going on?" he asked. "Has she changed her mind?"

"Just a little frozen feet," Elisha replied.

"It's cold feet," Kelsey said and tried not to laugh.

"You know what the hell I mean. I knew it was something like that. The way she took off running across the grass you would have sworn she had hot feet!" Elisha laughed. Joseph and Kelsey stared at her as if to ask, *how could you?* "Hey, I'm just trying to lighten the mood. I'm gonna go look for the make up artist." Elisha started on her way down the hall.

"As Elisha was trying to say, she had a little bit of cold feet. Everything is better now. She will be out. We need to get her put back together. I'm sure everyone is restless and concerned. You can go and let them know she will be back out soon," Kelsey said to Joseph.

"Are you sure she's coming out?" Joseph asked with a look of complete and utter concern.

Kelsey reassured him. "Yes. Now go on. You know it's bad luck to see the bride before the wedding, although technically you have already seen her."

Joseph went to calm the guests and reassure them that the wedding would still take place. Kelsey then peeped her head back in the restroom door to find Yvette staring at herself in the mirror.

"You look okay, girl. You ready to do this?"

"Yes," Yvette replied. "Just give me a minute alone."

"Okay girl, you better not disappear. I was understanding the first time, but I will be pissed if you pull that again. Besides, I have already told that man that you will be out there."

"No, I'm coming. I just need a moment alone."

"Okay then, I'm going to go and see if Elisha has found the makeup artist, then I will be right back."

All alone, Yvette reflected over her life. She thought about the unsuccessful relationships, and how she had fallen hard for the wrong guys, for all the wrong reasons. She had finally found someone who truly loved her. *How could she have almost messed that up? How could she embarrass herself and him like that? How can she go back out there and face everyone?* Elisha and Kelsey came back with the makeup artist.

"Okay, she's here. Let's get you together and get this show back on the road!" Elisha said.

"Hey, which one is Joseph's mother?" Kelsey asked.

"Oh, none of his family could make it and his mom has Alzheimer's, so it's just his co-workers and a few friends out there," Yvette responded.

"What kind of shit is that? You mean to tell me he has no family present?" Elisha asked.

"No, he doesn't and that's okay. All that matters is Joseph and I, and the commitment we make to each other today. I will meet her after the wedding."

"Okay, wait a goddamn minute. You have not met his mother, yet? Awwww, hell no. You haven't met the mom, no family is here to show support. I don't know, I just don't know," Elisha went on.

"Shut up, Elisha. Didn't you hear the girl say his mother has Alzheimer's?"

"I wouldn't care. Put her ass in a wheelchair and roll her ass to the front of the aisle, and feed her Goldfish crackers if she gets out of order. You know old people like Goldfish crackers, Fig Newtons, or something! She should be here. Somebody should be here for him."

"Did you just say feed the lady Goldfish crackers and Fig Newtons?" Kelsey laughed. The makeup artist began to work on Yvette's face. She did slight touch ups here and there where her mascara ran down her face due to her tears. She reapplied her lipstick while Yvette stared straight ahead into the mirror as though she had zoned out.

"Hey, hey!" Elisha said and snapped her fingers. "Snap out of it, bitch. This wedding is going down today. I'm not playing."

"Girl, I'm good. Just focused."

By the time Yvette and her two friends got themselves together, the coordinator and Yvette's father, was waiting by the door to restart the ceremony.

"It's okay, baby," her father said. "You know if you're not ready to do this you, don't have to and you shouldn't," he said as he looked into her eyes with fatherly concern.

"I'm fine, dad." In the back of her mind she thought, *I couldn't just walk away like that. Joseph is a good man. People have traveled near and far to be here for this day. There was a lot of money spent on dresses, the DJ, caterers, the venue, limousines, and much more.*

Yvette took a deep breath as the music began to play once more and she proceeded to walk towards the outside altar where her bridal party, Joseph, and the pastor waited. As she walked down the aisle, the looks on the faces of her family and friends gave her comfort. They seemed to say, "It's okay."

The wedding continued and Yvette and Joseph exchanged vows without fail. With tears in his eyes, Joseph professed his love for Yvette and they jumped the broom to symbolize the start of their new life together, leaving the past in the past, and proceeding with the future. The reception was amazing. There were lots of food, dancing, and laughter. Yvette did it again. She landed a husband once more and this time it seemed like she made the right choice. Joseph had "the look of love" in his eyes all night. Each time he looked at Yvette it showed and everyone saw it. During the reception they played the usual line dance songs ranging from The Electric Slide to the Cupid Shuffle. Everyone had a ball. Elisha and Kelsey made their way to the new couple's table.

Elisha bent down and whispered in Yvette's ear, "You good, Runaway Bride?" she chuckled.

"That's not funny Elisha. Stop it." Yvette managed to laugh.

"What's so funny?" Joseph asked.

"Oh, nothing, babe," Yvette replied.

"Excuse us for a minute while we borrow your new bride. We're going to go get our dance on. We will be right back."

"Okay, don't keep her too long," Joseph said and kissed Yvette's hand. The ladies pulled her toward the dance floor by the other hand.

"Girl, I was just playing," Elisha said once they got on the dance floor.

"I'm already embarrassed enough about it. Don't keep reminding me."

"I'm just saying, bitch, the way you left that altar and took off across that grass, I felt like I was Joseph. The way my money was set up for this wedding, sacrifices I made, and sugar daddies I had to spend time with when I didn't want to, oh your ass had to get married today!"

"Elisha!" Kelsey shouted.

"I'm just saying, it was a lot."

The trio talked while they danced on a makeshift floor outside and underneath a huge white tent. Purple wisteria, and amethyst flowers, with white lighting were draped everywhere.

"Can I have my bride back?" Joseph had made his way to the dance floor where the three ladies huddled.

"Of course you can," Kelsey said. "Our bad."

"Yeah, besides I need to go holla at your best man," Elisha stated. "He looked rather tasty in that tux."

"Oh, Lord, there she goes," Kelsey exclaimed. The two trotted off the dance floor and left the newlywed couple to dance. Joseph grabbed his new bride around her waist and pulled her close. "Make It Last Forever," by Keith Sweat was set to play as they caressed one another and swayed from side-to-side.

"Yvette, I thought I was going to lose you."

"I know. I can't say, 'I'm sorry' enough. I was afraid with everything I had been through, that I could be the woman you need. I'm not perfect, Joseph." Yvette lowered her head in shame. Joseph took his index finger and placed it under her chin and lifted her head to allow him to look in her eyes.

"None of us are perfect, but we can be perfect for each other. We can grow together and learn from one another."

This was marriage number two for her. She desperately wanted to make it work. She didn't want it to end up in divorce like the last time. How could she have almost let the thoughts in her head ruin this beautiful moment on such a gorgeous day? Yvette then rested her head on Joseph's chest as the music continued to play. Everything felt perfect. She could hear Joseph's heart beating through his tuxedo jacket. He was much taller than her, even with six inch heels on. He rested his chin gently on the top of her head. The exchange of energy was great and felt even better.

CHAPTER 2
BECOMING MRS. JENNINGS

In the beginning, Joseph moved into Yvette's home. It was easier that way since her place was a little bigger and provided more space. Although Jaden had graduated from high school, he still lived at home. Katrina would also come home during the summer break from college, as well as for the holidays. Joseph's small apartment would never accommodate them all. Still, this was only temporary. The plan was for them to search for an even bigger home, spacious enough for them all. Joseph and Yvette settled into married life pretty seamlessly and everything continued to flow well.

Katrina and Jaden felt odd having a man living in the house in their space after all this time. Geo, Yvette's former boyfriend, had spent nights, but it was never permanent. It definitely took some getting used to for everyone, including Yvette. Joseph was an outgoing guy. He was always looking for activities to do in the city, be it a concert, play, musical, or a night out on the town for dinner. Outside of Yvette's all ready full work calendar events, Joseph would always have something planned for them to do. That would include the children from time to time. This made Yvette feel great that he would include her children.

She would often come home and Jaden would be out and about with him looking at cars, shopping for clothes, or hanging out having men's talk, something she felt Jaden needed in his life.

Ever since Jaden turned 17, his father, Lawrence, seemed to almost disappear from their lives. He had remarried long before Yvette did, but he began a disappearing act during the dating process with his new wife. Jaden often struggled with the choice their father made not to be in their lives. After all, Yvette divorced him—that did not mean he was divorced from his children. Nevertheless, life goes on and Yvette was happy to have a father-figure for her children. Although they were almost grown, it was still welcomed.

Yvette came in from a long day at work. "Jaden are you here?" she called out. There was no answer. Jaden hadn't bought a car yet, therefore he utilized cab services to get to and from his job at a local fast food restaurant when he couldn't get Yvette to drop him off due to her work schedule. *I guess he's not here. He's probably either at work or with his girlfriend, Danica,* she thought. Yvette continued to her bedroom, got undressed, and proceeded to relax across the bed. Shortly thereafter, she heard the front door open and various rumblings.

"Mom, where you at?" Jaden called out.

"I'm in my room. Boy, stop yelling through the damn house!"

Jaden made his way into his mother's room. He carried multiple bags. Joseph following behind him.

"Hey, babe," Joseph said and kissed her on the forehead.

"Where have y'all been?" she asked.

Jaden poured clothing out of the bags of clothing on the bed.

"You took him shopping? He didn't need anything. He has plenty of clothes."

"We just spent some male bonding time. It was an opportunity for us to get to know each other more, babe, no big deal. So he already has clothes, now he has a few more."

As the months went on, Joseph, Yvette, and the children spent more time together. Things seemed to be going well. Joseph and Yvette began to look for a new home. After working with a real estate agent for some time, they finally decided on a house that was perfect for their new family. It was settled in a beautiful subdivision on a corner lot in Plano, Texas, which was one of the suburban areas outside of Dallas. The name of the subdivision was Whispering Lakes. The house they chose was around 4,000 sq ft. It included 4 bedrooms and 3 and ½ baths with a game room, a huge backyard for entertaining and a two car garage. Everything seemed to fall into place. Joseph consulted with Yvette on every aspect of the house because he wanted to make sure she was happy. Katrina was still away at college, nevertheless there was still a room waiting for her whenever she came home. In the meantime, it was the three of them, Joseph, Yvette, and Jaden.

CHAPTER 3
IN THE BEGINNING

Moving day came. Yvette invited Kelsey and Elisha over to help load up a few of the smaller items into their cars to take to the new house, while Joseph was at work, as a recruiter for the US Army. Once Joseph got off, he and a few friends would get together and use a rental truck to move the heavier furniture and appliances, etc.

"Let me say this first and foremost," Elisha started with a ghetto smack of her lips. "Let this be the last time we have to come over and pack, unpack, or move any damn thing when it comes to a man again. Okay?"

"Really, Elisha," Kelsey said.

"Yes, bitch really, shit! What you mean?"

"Girl, if this shit don't work out, we will move your ass again. That's what we do!"

Kelsey said, "Speak for your damn self. If you have any doubts, you better stay in your own house. Why y'all so in a hurry to move? This house is big enough. Y'all haven't been married a year yet. You know men change. Once they feel like they have you 100% … ."

"Stop it, Elisha! Stop being a Negative Nancy," Kelsey warned. "Besides, not all men are the same. Joseph is different. He's a God-fearing man. He works hard. He doesn't exclude her children and seems to really and truly love her."

"Okay guys, we are not going to argue about my husband. I need you to help me get this stuff moved."

15

"Thank you, Elisha for your concern, but all is well. My husband loves me and I love him. We are good," Yvette stated.

Yvette and the two ladies gathered small items they can fit in their cars and proceeded on to the new house. Once inside the new house, Kelsey and Elisha stood in awe of its massive size. There was a grand entryway with a sweeping staircase. The two-story home had french doors to the rear, accompanied by an elegant formal dining room, tremendous chef's kitchen, den/family room with a marble fireplace and glass doors to the backyard, a home office, and a game room upstairs. The divine master suite had tray ceilings, massive windows, plush carpet throughout, and separate showers with a Jacuzzi tub and his and her sinks.

"Why do you need this much house? It's just the three of you?" Kelsey asked.

"It's what Joseph wanted. Besides, if he pisses me off, it's big enough for me to have my own space for a minute without seeing him."

"What would be even better is you not giving up your own house just yet and try this out for a while to see how it really works," Elisha said.

"What is your problem?" Yvette asked. "What's with the Negative Nancy bullshit? We are married now. It's not like we're dating still. There's no halfway in and halfway out. It's all or nothing."

"Are you sure you are in now, because your ass ran pretty fast across that grass?" Elisha laughed. Yvette was not amused. Her face went blank and she didn't crack a smile.

"Why would you bring that up?" Kelsey asked.

"It was a fucking joke," Elisha said harshly.

"Why now, though, Elisha?" Yvette asked. "That is over and done with. You wanna bring up some more humiliating moments I've endured? You want your fucking money back for your dress, your shoes, and the day you took off work because that's all you have talked about and frankly I'm tired of hearing about it!" Yvette yelled.

"I don't want you to end up in a bad situation that's all. You and Kelsey didn't tell me anything about the engagement and I was barely included in the wedding plans."

"You are so negative that's why!"

"No, I'm real, Yvette. I don't think you were fully over some situations, if you know what I mean," Elisha said with an eyebrow raised. "You jumped into this relationship with Joseph without complete closure."

"You know what, Elisha? I think you're jealous," Yvette stated.

"Jealous?" Elisha yelled. "What the fuck?"

"Yes! All you like to do is party and mess around on your husband, but I guess that shit is going to get really boring because you have one less person to ride out with you every time you want to get out, now that I'm married!"

"Bitch, I don't need anyone to ride out with me, I roll solo with no problem!"

"Ladies, ladies. What's going on here? It is not that serious!" Kelsey yelled. "Let's not do this. We are better than this."

"It wasn't that serious, but it is now," Elisha said.

She dropped the boxes she held and turned to storm out of the door. Before she left, she had a few final words.

"I hope for your sake that you make it last forever like the Keith Sweat song y'all danced to said. You have a tendency to constantly place small bandages over gaping wounds, and ignore the breakthrough bleeding. I know who I am. I don't make excuses for myself or my marriage and I'll be damned if I pretend!"

With those words Elisha walked out, got into her car and drove away. Kelsey and Yvette stood in the huge foyer with high vaulted ceilings that had a skylight where the sun shined through and bounced around on the limestone marble flooring.

"Yvette, she's just concerned for you that's all," Kelsey said.

"Us running the streets with her is the only thing that makes her happy. Now there's one less of us to club with and she's pissed," Yvette replied. "Not even you really, because you're not that big on clubbing. We would have to practically pry you out of the house sometimes, so that really means she will be rolling solo for the most part."

"I still feel her concern is genuine. Heck I'm even a little concerned. I want you to be happy."

"Don't be concerned. I'm in a good place and I'm happy with a great husband. I mean, look at this house. What more can I ask for?" Yvette exclaimed as she looked around her beautiful home.

Kelsey had many thoughts in the back of her mind and several things she wanted to say, but she didn't want to end up on the outs with Yvette like Elisha.

"Okay, girl let's get the rest of these boxes from the car moved in. I'm on a time schedule," Kelsey said. They headed outside to their vehicles.

"Girl, you must be trying to go see that man before Edward gets off, huh?"

"Maybe," Kelsey said with a slight grin.

"Girl, you are almost as bad as Elisha."

"Well, if Edward had never cheated to begin with, which caused us to separate, I would have never met Raheem." She popped the trunk of her car and retrieved a few items.

"When you two got back together, I thought it was supposed to stop."

Yvette reached behind the seat of her vehicle and struggled to remove one of the boxes.

"Yeah it was supposed to and now I can't."

"What do you mean you can't? You can if you really want to."

Yvette looked at her with disbelief at the words, "I can't."

"Just trust me, I can't. Especially not right now."

"I'm not understanding. What do you mean, especially not right now?" Yvette put the box on the ground. Kelsey took a deep breath.

"I'm pregnant and I don't know if it's Edward's or Raheem's."

"Oh, my God!" Yvette said with her mouth wide open. Her eyes looked like they were the size of two ping pong balls. "Who would you like to be the father?"

"I really want it to be, and I think Raheem is the father. We have been going at it like crazy, and Edward and I may have had sex once a week, if that.

"What are you going to do, Kelsey, seriously?"

"In my heart, I honestly feel like it's Raheem's. He told me he wanted me to have his baby so if it is, I'm leaving Edward for him."

"Are you fucking crazy!" Yvette asked in complete disappointment. She almost dropped the box she carried into the house. "That man already has five kids and he lives with his kids' mother. Kelsey how could you be so naive? You are too old to make that kind of mistake. Your children and my children are practically the same age. Why would you want to start over under these type of circumstances?"

"Oh, and you're so perfect, right?" Kelsey shouted.

"No," Yvette said. "Look, Elisha has already left here pissed off. I'm not trying to make you mad, too. I'm concerned, that's all. Just like you were concerned for me."

"No need to be concerned. I got it under control, trust me," Kelsey replied.

"Okay, girl, well let's get the rest of these things out of the car."

"Awww, shit!" Yvette said.

"What?" Kelsey asked.

"Elisha still has some of my things in her car."

"That just means you have to talk to her again now."

"Depending on what it is, not really," Yvette said casually.

"Don't be like that. We're girls, and first and foremost, we are family. You all have to talk eventually, besides it's not that serious."

"I hear you. Anyways, let's at least get this done before Joseph and the guys come with the truck and we are still here and haven't done much at all."

CHAPTER 4
RED FLAGS

With the move behind them, Joseph returned to his weekly activities. He always had an outing or two planned. "Hey, I got tickets to the Charlie Wilson concert tomorrow night," Joseph said as he came in from a long day at work. He threw his keys on the kitchen counter and kissed Yvette on the forehead as she peeled potatoes for the night's dinner.

"Sounds great. Oh, you know I love me some Uncle Charlie," she said and kissed him on the lips with gratitude.

"What are you cooking?" he asked.

"Ummmm, just a little something something—meatloaf, mashed potatoes, dinner rolls, broccoli with cheese and fresh baked red velvet cake."

"That sounds like a lot of something," he laughed. "Sounds delicious. I can't wait!"

"Yeah, I cooked some broccoli to go with it because I know how much Jaden likes it with meatloaf."

"So is this dinner for Jaden or is it for me?" Joseph asked with a stern look on his face.

"It's for all of us," Yvette responded. "I tried to cook something that I thought we all would like."

"Hmmm, that you felt everyone would like or Jaden? I don't recall telling you that any of these things were my favorite." Joseph then walked away and went into the master bedroom which was adjacent to the huge living room. Yvette stood in the kitchen with a look of shock on her face. *What the hell just happened?* The night went on and the trio had dinner, but Yvette still thought about Joseph's earlier remarks. It was unlike him. After dinner, Yvette and Joseph retreated into the bedroom. Yvette showered and then climbed into bed with an already showered Joseph. She was determined to address her concerns about the conversation.

"Hey, babe," she started. "I want to talk to you about the comment you made earlier when you came home from work about dinner."

"Awww, babe, I was just tired."

"But I just … ." she started again.

"Yvette!" Joseph said abruptly. "There's nothing to discuss."

He turned over, signaling the end of the conversation. Yvette did not want to cause an argument. She did the same. She hated being cut off and not being able to express herself but she let it be. Although it would remain tucked away in her mind for now, she knew she had to address it at some point.

Around 12 am, she awakened to Joseph's warm lips kissing her lower back as she lay on her side, with her back facing him. His lips made their way to her hips, kissing slowly and repeatedly. Yvette still held a grudge for not being able to get a clear and concise understanding for his disgruntled comments. She laid there and pretended to be unfazed by the feel of his wet, soft lips gently kissing her body. She wore a pink cotton tank top with a pair of lacy white panties that laid just right across the cheeks of her voluptuous ass. It was enough to wake the dead from years of slumber if they could see it. As he continued to kiss her body, he made his way down her thighs then to the back of her knees where he licked slowly and seductively. She could hardly hold her composure. He made his way back up her thighs then he rolled her over on her back and looked into her eyes without saying a word. A full moon shone through the sheer curtains that covered the floor to ceiling windows in their enormous bedroom and landed across her face just enough so that their eyes would meet in the darkness. They still did not say a word to each other. Joseph slowly removed her panties. In the back of the her mind she said, *oh you want to fuck but we can't talk about my concerns,* while the other part screamed, *yes!* Somewhat reluctantly, Yvette moved her hips from one side to the other, aiding Joseph in the removal of her panties. Once removed, Joseph cupped both hands underneath her ample behind and dragged her body down so that she was aligned in a perfect, no hands, pussy buffet position. Yvette still tried to appear unfazed as he looked up at her to make eye contact and winked as if to say, *I know you're mad but you will get over it in 5 4 3 2 1.* Joseph dove in face-first into her heavenly peach. His hot wet tongue moved feverishly back and forth and fully enveloped every fold and crevice. Yvette could no longer hold on to her gripe. She gave in to her yes. She grabbed a handful of Joseph's dreads as she arched her back and released all of her desires.

A passionate sex session ensued until they both fell asleep. It wasn't long but it was enough to take the edge off. Although she was a sucker for great sex, it did not negate the fact of what Joseph did earlier in the day but she would let it go for now. The following day was the start of the weekend as well as the day of the concert. Yvette went to work as usual with plans to leave early so she could have plenty of time to prepare and look her finest next to her man that night.

During work the next day, she received a call from Joseph.

"Hey, babe," Yvette answered.

"Hey, love of my life. How are things going at work today?" Joseph asked.

"Everything is going good. I can't wait for the concert tonight. It's been a minute since we had a date night.

Everything has been work, work, work, and getting the house situated."

"Yeah, I know. Look, babe, I know you're working hard. I'm out looking for something to wear tonight so I thought I would pick up something for you, too."

"Aww, honey you don't have to do that. I have plenty of things in the closet that I can wear."

"I know you do, but I see a few things that I would like to see you in."

"Okay, babe, I know you have good taste. Whatever you like, I trust you."

Yvette got off the phone and felt a little impressed and special that her man wanted to shop for her something nice to wear that night. She went back to her work day. Throughout the course of the day, Joseph texted her different pictures of outfits and accessories he liked and wanted to see her in until they came to an agreement. They agreed on a simple but sexy black halter top dress that dipped low in the rear and exposed her entire back all the way down to her waistline, along with a pair of sexy peep-toe slingback 6 inch stiletto pumps. Yvette rushed straight home after work with only an hour and a half to get ready. Joseph was already home getting himself together.

"Hey, babe," Yvette said and kissed him in a haste and then ran off to the shower. When Yvette got out of the shower, Joseph was already dressed. He stood 6 ft tall in a pair of black slacks and a button-down off-white shirt that was form-fitted and tapered in the waist slightly to show off his fit body. A silver Movado watch with a blue face and matching bracelet adorned his wrist. His dreads were freshly twisted and draped down his back and he had a diamond stud in one ear. Yvette took one look and began to drown in his essence. She also became intoxicated from the smell of his cologne. "Boy you almost make me want to say, 'cancel the concert and you can perform for me right here and now!'"

"Oh, you like what you see, huh?" he said with a sly smirk.

"Yes, I do," she said and looked at him seductively and traced her index finger down the center of his chest. He kissed her on the lips and gave her a love pat on her butt.

"Come on, Bae, get dressed. We're going to be late. I will take care of you when we get back. I promise."

"Let me hurry and put this dress on so I can hurry and get back and take it off!" she said with a wink. Then off she went into the walk-in closet which also doubled as a changing room for Yvette because it was huge. She came out with the dress that hugged her in all the right places. She did a quick makeup beat—red lips and lashes, a slight tossell of her wavy shoulder-length hair extensions and she was ready. Her coco smooth dark skin didn't require much as it was practically flawless.

Once the pair arrived at the concert they waited in line to grab a few drinks before taking their seats. Joseph made sure he got the best tickets. They were not too close to the stage but they were close enough. While they waited in line, a woman walked over to Yvette and complimented her on her entire outfit.

"Thank you," Yvette replied.

Joseph turned around from the counter. He handed a drink to Yvette and kept the other one for himself.

"What did she say?" he asked.

"Oh, she was complimenting me on my outfit." After she explained to him, somehow Yvette fumbled her drink and she accidentally spilled some of it on his hands, and a little on his sleeve. Yvette rushed over to the counter and grabbed some napkins to dry his hand and sleeve. "Thank God we are drinking clear liquor tonight, otherwise that would have been a nasty stain and we haven't even gotten inside yet. There, there. All cleaned up. Don't say I've never done anything for you," Yvette joked.

"What?" Joseph asked abruptly.

"I said 'don't ever say I didn't do anything for you.' It's a joke, babe."

"You getting me a napkin and me spending all day shopping for you doesn't compare. That's why you got a compliment tonight, because of me."

"Are you serious? I was just joking with you." Yvette stared at him in disbelief.

"Yeah, I was too," he replied smartly.

Yvette was taken aback. She didn't know how to respond. She thought, *is this motherfucker serious?* She didn't want to make a scene. She internalized her feelings for the sake of the night although she was burning up on the inside. One of her pet peeves has always been when someone does something for you then throws it in your face. That ran her red hot. Yvette managed to hold her tongue and get through the concert. Charlie Wilson put on a hell of a show and sang all of his famous hits from, "You Dropped a Bomb on Me" to "Outstanding," and "My Heart is Yearning for Your Love."

When the last song played, Joseph grabbed Yvette's hand and sang in her ear. Yvette still fumed from his sly remark and she forced a smile to appease him. She couldn't wait to get home and rip that dress from her body and throw the shoes back in the box. She would never give him the opportunity to say that to her again! The night went on and Yvette got through it with fake smiles and grins. On the way home, Yvette was quiet. Joseph noticed it.

"What's wrong, babe? Why are you so quiet? Did you enjoy yourself?"

"Yes, I did," she responded but sat with her arms folded. She stared straight ahead through the windshield.

"Can a brother get a smile or even a thank you?"

Yvette turned and looked at him angrily and said, "I want to thank you in advance for never speaking about what you have done for me or do for me! If you want to do something for me, do it. Don't throw it in my face, otherwise you can keep it!"

"What are you talking about?" Joseph asked. He seemed to be genuinely confused and concerned that Yvette was upset. Joseph had totally moved on from that moment, but apparently Yvette had not.

"I'm talking about you talking about how you shopped for me and bought tickets for the concert!"

"Oh my God, you still on that? Let it go, Bae. We had a good evening."

"Whatever," she replied with her arms still folded. She looked out of the passenger side window with nothing more to say. Joseph looked at her with dismay, shook his head, and continued the drive home.

The next morning she was still a little upset but managed to let It go. Of course she had a little morning sexual encouragement from Joseph. She had awakened to the feel of his soft lips kissing her on her inner thighs, then using nothing but his tongue to slide her panties to the side, he gave, himself breakfast in bed compliments of Chateau de Yvette. Although she was a little resistant at first with every hot, wet, stroke of his tongue she could not help but let go. The morning relieved some of the tension from last night's fortuity.

As Yvette relaxed in the aftermath, still not really saying much to Joseph, he asked, "Are you still upset with me?"

"No, I'm good," Yvette replied. That was basically woman code for "Yeah, I'm still pissed but I'm gonna let you make it for now." Her body language said the same.

"I didn't mean anything by it. I wanted you to have a beautiful night, look great, and feel even better. Please forgive me." Joseph laid there with his head on Yvette's stomach and looked up at her, with his dreadlocks disheveled all over his head. He managed to still look sexy. Yvette could not resist looking into those almond-shaped and slightly chinky eyes.

She replied, "Yes, I forgive you."

"Thanks, baby, now gimme a kiss," he said.

He raised up to meet her lips with his.

Yvette gave him her cheek to kiss.

"You don't want to kiss me on my lips?" Joseph chuckled. "It's your juices. I just finished tasting you."

"It's not that," Yvette explained. "I have morning breath."

"I don't care," he replied." He grabbed her by the back of her head and forced his lips onto hers. "Taste good doesn't it? Now you know why I enjoy it so much."

With that, Joseph got up and went into the bathroom to shower and shave for work. Yvette's phone rang. It was Katrina. This was her sophomore year in college. She seemed to be better adjusted.

"Hey, hun. What's going on?" she asked her daughter.

"Hey, Mom, everything is going okay," although her voice didn't sound okay.

"What's wrong?" Yvette asked.

"You don't sound like yourself."

"My new roommate this semester is giving me the blues. Last night I came home from work and there were two guys and a girl hanging out in the room. They were sitting on my bed and playing loud music. I just wanted to study, shower, and sleep."

"So what did you do about it, Katrina?"

"I went down to the common area and studied."

"What?" Yvette shouted. "Why the hell would you leave your own damn room?" Katrina was a passive, non-confrontational, introvert type. She was the total opposite of her mother. "I can't believe you left your damn room. I'm paying for you to be there. Why didn't you ask them to leave?"

"I didn't want to start any confusion. Besides they seemed ghetto."

"I don't give a damn!" Yvette shouted.

"Mom, calm down."

"Don't tell me to calm down. You know how I get when you don't stick up for yourself!"

"Mom, I got it under control," Katrina replied.

"Okay, if you say so. I'm done with it. You calling me and upsetting my nerves with this and expect me not to react. I got to go. I have a lot of things on my mind already today. I will talk to you later. I love you."

"I love you, too, Mom. Trust me. I'm okay. I will handle it on my own."

They hung up the phone. Yvette still fumed. She hated that she could no longer be there to protect her but she had to let her grow up and handle things her way.

"Who were you yelling at?" Joseph asked as he came out of the bathroom still dripping wet from the shower but wrapped in a towel.

"Just a little situation with Katrina at school. It's no big deal."

"You need another dose of the attitude adjuster?" he said with a smirk as he removed his towel and exposed his naked loins. Yvette was not amused but she was careful not to show it on her face.

"No, honey, I'm good," she replied. "You sure? I got about three minutes to spare."

Yvette smiled as she thought, *yeah, exactly three minutes indeed.*

"No, I'm going to shower and get dressed, too. I'm going to hang out with Kelsey today since I'm off. I hadn't seen her since she helped us move in."

"Okay," Joseph replied. Enjoy yourself. You will be home by the time I get off work right?"

"I should be."

"I hope so." His response made Yvette feel some type of way but she chose to ignore it and go into the bathroom and shower.

CHAPTER 5
GIRLS WILL BE GIRLS

Kelsey and Yvette decided they would meet for happy hour at Club Ignite. Everything was half off from 3 pm to 6 pm, drinks, wings, hookah, you name it. Still, Yvette was leery about meeting there. She had not been there since she had gotten married. Everything she did lately was with Joseph. Kelsey could have picked another place to meet, nevertheless, Yvette obliged her. She was all dolled up in a yellow peplum top with a pair of damaged denim capris and tan wedge heels, hair and makeup, on point.

"Hey, chica," Kelsey said as she came to the door with drinks in both hands. I got you your first drink and we are sitting in our old spot."

A lot about the place had changed in the months Yvette had not been there... oh, it was almost a year now. Nevertheless, she still saw some familiar faces hanging around.

"Girl, why you looking around like that? It's almost the same look you had the first time you came here after your divorce."

"Just checking the scenery," Yvette responded. "Why did you want to come here, Kelsey, out of all places?"

"Girl, this was our spot and you know it. We had some great times here!"

"Yeah, we did."

"Don't say it like that. You were engaged here."

In an instant, a movie reel began to play in Yvette's mind of that night. More specifically, she saw the looks on the faces of Dalvin and Mitchell during the proposal. The looks were etched in her memory forever.

Kelsey's phone rang. "I'm in the back where we used to sit," she answered.

"Who else did you invite?" Yvette asked. "Don't tell me you...?" and before she could finish, she looked up and there was Elisha.

"Bitch, no you did not set this up," Elisha said as she approached the table. She and Yvette had not spoken since the day Yvette moved into her new house and they had the disagreement.

"And on that note, I'm leaving," Yvette said. She grabbed her purse and began to leave.

"No," Kelsey said. "We have been friends for way too long and family even longer. This is stupid. There is no reason why you two should not be able to talk this out. We have done a lot together, good and bad. Sit down, Yvette."

Kelsey pulled Yvette's purse out of her hand. "Y'all are so stubborn it's crazy. Come on Elisha. Sit down and let's fix this." Reluctantly, the two sat down. They were stone-faced and did not say a word. "Come on, say something," Kelsey implored.

"Okay," Elisha started. "How's married life?"

"It's great," Yvette responded with a tight lip.

"Oh, my damn. Waiter can you please bring me a double shot of Patrón please? These heifers are going to drive me crazy today."

"Why are you drinking" Yvette asked. "And you're pregnant?"

"Bitch, what?" Elisha shouted.

"Damn, girl. I hadn't told anyone but you! Big mouth!"

"I know you fucking lying," Elisha said with her hand over her mouth. "Who's the Pappy?" she said sarcastically. All three of them laughed.

"If that's what it took to get your asses to break the ice, then fine, I will take that at my expense, and besides the drinks are not for me. They are for y'all bitter bitches," she chuckled. "Because y'all need to relax."

"No, but for real though whose is it?" Elisha asked sincerely.

"Honestly," Kelsey said as she looked down then up again at Yvette and Elisha. "I don't know. I want it to be Raheem's."

"Bitch why? You think that's going to make him leave his family? You been creeping with this bastard for a few years now helping him get established and ducking in and out of hotels. Why would you let this happen?"

"Look, Elisha, I'm sure she didn't plan this, right Kelsey?" Kelsey stared at the two of them. "Right, Kelsey?" Yvette asked the question once more intensely.

"He said he wanted me to have his baby," Kelsey finally responded.

"Bitch! Are you crazy!" Elisha shouted! "You did this shit on purpose? Waiter, yes, over here. Can you hurry and make that four double shots of Patrón, please? Hell, just bring us the bottle, some salt, and a lot of lime. Please, and thank you."

"You are playing a dangerous game," Yvette said. "Have you told Edward yet?"

"Yes, I told him I'm pregnant but he thinks it's his. I didn't tell him about the possibility."

"Wow!" Yvette was stunned.

"He was doing his thing when we were separated and I was doing mine."

"But you still see Raheem on and off and you two have moved back and are trying to make things work," Yvette stated.

"Are you judging me?" Kelsey asked.

"Not at all. I'm just saying because you know we all have skeletons."

"Bitch, some skeletons are dead. You got live skeletons in your closet, bitch!" Elisha laughed.

"How in the hell can you have a live skeleton, crazy ass girl?" Yvette laughed.

"You see why I didn't tell her ass anything? She takes everything for a joke," Kelsey said. "Honey, lighten up. May as well laugh about it instead of crying about it. What's done is done and you chose it so let's drink and enjoy. I'm over this shit."

The DJ played the "wobble," song. "Oh, that's my shit right there!" Elisha said and jumped up after downing her double shot of Patrón. She headed to the dance floor. "Come on bitches, It's just like the good old days. Let's get it. Come on and wobble. Kelsey that's what you are going to be doing in the next few months anyway with a big ass belly," Elisha laughed hysterically.

"I can't stand her ass," Kelsey said.

"It was your idea to invite her, now come on, let's wobble," Yvette said as she headed to the dance floor and pulled Kelsey by the hand. The threesome was back together again. It was like old times. One song led to another and one drink led to another. Before they knew it, time had passed extremely fast.

"Oh, God," Yvette exclaimed. It's almost 9 o' clock. I need to get my ass home. I told Joseph I would be there by the time he got home."

"What time does he get home?" Kelsey asked.

"Usually around 7 or 7:30."

"Oops!" Kelsey replied.

"Uh oh, you in trouble, bitch," Elisha taunted with her hand over her mouth. She laughed.

"Girl, I'm grown," Yvette stated firmly.

"I see you gathering your shit to go," Elisha countered.

"Yes, because it's time. This happy hour went way over the expected time. It had been a long time since we all hung out together. We were having fun," Kelsey said. "But yeah, go ahead and get home. We don't want your marriage to be jacked up like ours."

"Hold up, sis," Elisha said. "My marriage is perfectly okay. We have an understanding that works for us."

"Yeah, okay," Kelsey remarked. "As long as what's outside doesn't cross over into the inside right?"

"You fucking right!" Elisha, said, profoundly nodding her head.

"How can you live like that? Marriage is supposed to be a sacred union between two people who are united under God's word," Yvette stated.

"Don't start with that holier-than-thou shit like you're so innocent now," Elisha said aggressively.

"I'm not saying I am but one thing I can honestly say is that I take my marriage seriously and my vows before God seriously," Yvette responded.

"Oh, really well good for you. How seriously does your husband take his vows?" Elisha asked, as if she knew something Yvette didn't.

"What the fuck is that supposed to mean?" Yvette asked.

"I'm simply saying, maybe you should have looked deep before you leaped."

"You know what? I'm going to leave. Your ass is miserable even though you act like you're okay in this quote-unquote open marriage. You're actually miserable and you want everyone to be miserable right along with you. Staying out all night in the clubs meeting men and using them as substitutes for what you're not getting from your husband!"

"Stop it!" Kelsey yelled. "Damn, we all just got back on one accord. Let's not do this ladies."

"Fuck her," Yvette exclaimed. She grabbed her purse and stormed out of the club.

"Elisha! Why would you say something like that? Do you know something about Joseph?"

"All I'm going to say is she probably should have kept running that day."

"What?" Kelsey said. She was puzzled.

"That's all I'm going to say for now."

"Girl, you can't make a brash statement like that out of the blue with nothing behind it."

"Oh, there's something behind it, trust me."

"Oh, my God. I don't even want to know. Let's go. I finally got you to talking and having fun and there you go messing it up. Let's go girl."

"Whatever. In time she will see, if she hasn't already started to see."

CHAPTER 6
A WOLF IN SHEEP'S CLOTHING

Arriving home that night, Yvette was frustrated overall with the catty drama with Elisha. She pulled into the garage and of course, Joseph was already home. She opened the door, walked into the living area, and threw her keys into a purple glass bowl that sat on a table in her foyer and hung her purse on the coat stand that stood next to it. Using the corner of the table to steady herself, she took her shoes off one by one. In the distance, she could hear the sounds of the television in the master bedroom. She held her shoes in her hand and walked to the bedroom. When she entered, she saw Joseph sitting up. He was wide awake with his shirt off and the light from the TV bounced off his bare chest in the dark while he stared straight ahead. He didn't even acknowledge the fact that she had walked into the room. He flipped through the channels and finally spoke.

"I thought you said you would be here by the time I got home?

Yvette replied, "Yeah I know. Time got away from me. You know it had been a minute since I hung out with the girls." Yvette leaned in to give Joseph a kiss but he remained stone-faced and continued to channel surf. He did not turn towards her to receive her affection. "So you're mad now?" Yvette asked. She was astonished by Joseph's coldness towards her.

"No I'm not mad. I'm disappointed that you would let two women that have nothing going on for themselves keep you out past the time you said you would be home with your husband."

"How do you know what they have going on?" Yvette responded defensively.

"The streets talk, Yvette. You have one friend who is a bona fide whore and will fuck anything that moves or has a dick. The other one is so hung up on the next woman's man, instead of her own husband, she doesn't even realize her own daughter is an undercover lesbian."

"What? How dare you? Where are you getting this information from?"

"It doesn't matter where I get it from, but that's who you chose to stay out with."

"Wow!" Yvette responded. "The last time I checked, I was a grown-ass woman. And why do you concern yourselves with other people's marriages anyway?" This was a side of Joseph she had never seen before or could have ever imagined.

"I'm not concerning myself. Like I said, the streets talk."

"Whatever. I'm going to take a shower."

Yvette went into the bathroom, turned the shower on full blast, undressed, and stepped in. While she was in the shower, she couldn't help but wonder where Joseph was getting all of this information from. She lathered and rinsed herself from head to toe. She reflected back on Elisha's statement as well. *What exactly did she mean, 'I should have looked deep before I leaped?'* She quickly disregarded the thought and said to herself, *she's just a miserable bitch looking for a partner to ride with her on the miserable bitch train, but I'm not buying any tickets.*

Yvette stepped out of the shower, dried herself off, then went into her enormous walk-in closet inside her bathroom. This closet was so huge there was a sitting area inside of it. She could get completely dressed and never leave the bathroom to do so. There was a dresser inside that held her lingerie and undergarments. It had her favorite sleep attire as well as various sweet smelling fragrances to douse all over her body to tempt her man's appetite. She was still upset by Joseph's attitude so she decided against the lingerie as well as her usual T-shirt and boy shorts. Instead she opted for an old over sized T-shirt that she loved. It was kind of tattered and came down to her knees but it was extremely comfortable. Underneath she would wear a pair of granny panties that she normally wore when it was that time of the month. She didn't spray on any Victoria's Secret fragrances or anything. One could only vaguely detect the smell of Oil of Olay lavender body wash. Yvette walked out of the bathroom and headed for bed.

Joseph took one look at her and said, "Oh, I guess you have an attitude now, being as though you got your don't-touch-me-because-I'm pissed-off clothes on. I know that has to be the case because you're not on your period — that was two weeks ago."

"Look Joseph. I'm not trying to debate with you. I'm going to sleep. I got to work in the morning."

"There would be no debate and you wouldn't be wearing that shit if you had been home on time with your husband."

"What the fuck you mean on time!" Yvette said angrily.

"I'm not a child nor do I have a curfew. You would think that I came home at 1 am or something. I got here at 10:30!"

"Watch your tone when you are talking to me," Joseph warned.

Yvette looked at Joseph, rolled over, and turned her back on him, but something in his tone resonated with her. It was a feeling she had never felt before.

A few hours later, Yvette was awakened by wet kisses on her inner thighs and a gentle tugging at her panties. Joseph had awakened in an aroused state about 4 am and it didn't matter to him what she was wearing.

"Joseph, I don't feel like it," she said and held on to her underwear to prevent him from removing them. "I have two hours before I have to get up for work," she said groggily.

"So, you are going to deny your husband?" Joseph said and looked up at her as he lay between her legs. Yvette eyes connected with him in the moonlight. She slowly released her grip and allowed him to appease himself. Besides it wouldn't last long anyway. You see, although Joseph, was decently endowed, his stroke game was more like a 50-yard dash instead of a marathon each time, unlike Dalvin or Geo. He had many other qualities though that the other two lacked. Although Yvette had an insatiable sexual appetite, and Joseph on occasion could not satisfy her, she made it work for the most part, by getting prepared beforehand with a glass of Chardonnay, which was the worst possible thing she could do. She never did understand what it was about Chardonnay and sex when it came to her. All she knew was that with one glass, her sex drive would skyrocket. Moments like this, when Joseph would wake her up in the wee hours of the morning and she couldn't get to that glass of Chardonnay, she would envision past moments with Dalvin or Geo to get to the level of ecstasy for her to release quickly. Sad but true. It was a horrible thing to engage in, but what else was she supposed to do?

There were times when she almost called out one of their names. There were other times when she desired to be gently choked while having a hard thrust back and forth against her body. Or even to have some thug-type shit whispered in her ear while being bent over doggy style and taking inches upon inches from the back. Instead, she married the sophomoric sex style of a man who like to make love all the time in a nice, slow, and gentle way. Yvette had to constantly remind herself of the qualities and attributes that Joseph possessed other than sexual. He slid her panties off and tried to excite her loins with a tantalizing tongue tango with her clitoris. Yvette really wasn't feeling it. She still held on to the animosity from earlier. It made it impossible for her to be in tune with her husband's desires. Once the tango ended, Joseph raised up and wiped his mouth that contained Yvette's lady juices, with his hands. He mounted her and the 50-yard dash began. From the beginning, she was not in the mood, therefore, she had to resort to one of her previous encounters to reach her peak. It was necessary for her husband to feel like he was completely satisfying her. It wasn't as though Joseph was bad in bed, or lacked endowment. He was just so straight-laced and short-winded than her norm. Nevertheless, she chose status, love, and stability over her sexual desires.

As Joseph thrust his body against Yvette, she began to replay a movie of thoughts in her head that starred none other than Dalvin. Why did she choose him to reach her sexual gratification with her husband? He was the man who hurt her more than any man ever in her life. He was the man she fell hard for and the one she never sought complete closure from. Although she moved on and was over him for the most part, she still yearned for that bad boy image of Geo and the swagger and confidence of Dalvin. With each stroke she envisioned Dalvin's face, his manipulative forehead kisses, his deep brown bedroom eyes, and succulent lips centered in the middle of a well-trimmed goatee. She closed her eyes, arched her back and took her husband in fully as she ran her nails down his back. She reminisced about the smell of Geo's cologne that would almost immediately send her hormones into a violent sexual rage. She desired the aggression of a long sexual encounter she knew she would receive from these men that would have her in a sexual haze for days after. Just as her husband began to near the finish line, she delved deep into her thoughts and could hear Dalvin's voice in her ear saying in his usual, sensual, provocative, and manipulative deep tone, "give me all of this pussy," as his hot lips and wet tongue licked her ear and caressed her neck.

Flashes of these thoughts caused her to climax and release harder than she had in a long time. As her body began to convulse uncontrollably, she began to cry out in passion.

Her husband felt like a champion, and Yvette felt sexually gratified. She also felt guilty that she had to resort to such measures to be able to reach sexual satisfaction with her husband. That part of her life was over. She was supposed to enjoy her new life free of drama and love unreturned or a dangerous kind of love. She traded it all in for real love, stability, protection, truth and love that was returned to her equally. Or did she?

Yvette woke up right before daybreak with a full bladder. She threw back the covers from her body and headed to the bathroom and noticed that her husband was not in bed. She relieved her bladder and in the quiet of the night she could hear a conversation in the distance. Her ears perked up and she listened and followed the conversation she heard. The voice sounded familiar and after a minute she realized it was Joseph talking in a totally different tone. It even sounded like a different language. She followed the conversation to the living room then realized it was coming from the outdoor patio area. It was indeed Joseph, but what was this language he was speaking? And who was he talking to? Yvette tiptoed hurriedly back to the bedroom as she heard Joseph shuffling around on the patio as though he was coming back inside. Hurrying across the living room and back into the bedroom, she stubbed her pinky toe on the foot of the bed. She gripped it in pain and put her hand over her mouth to silence the agony she felt from hitting her toe. She quietly slid back in bed and positioned herself as if she was asleep on her side with her back facing away from Joseph with the covers tucked under her chin. She could hear Joseph coming back into the room and carefully sliding into bed as he tried not to wake her. He snuggled up behind her and spooned with her. He wrapped his arms around her waist, his breath inhaling and exhaling on the back of her neck. Yvette lay there with her eyes wide open in the dark wondering *what the hell?* And Joseph lay there never the wiser that she had listened to his conversation.

A part of her wanted to question him badly but she decided to wait until morning. Nevertheless, she could barely sleep. As darkness turned to daylight, she awakened and resumed the normality of getting dressed for work. Yvette tried to find the words to begin a conversation that would allow her to ask Joseph about the newfound language he spoke that she had never heard before. The conversation never came about. The pair got dressed for work, briefly kissed one another goodbye and off to their nine-to-fives, they went. En route to work, she could not get the conversation she overheard out of her mind. Why had Joseph not told her he was from another country or whatever? Why was he hiding this from her? Then the comment Elisha made dawned on her. *Maybe she should have looked deep before she leaped. Hmmmm* she thought to herself. *What does she know that I don't know?*

Being that Elisha was always in the streets partying, she was privy to the latest gossip and always in everyone's business instead of taking care of her own. Although they had fallen out and had a huge disagreement the last time they saw one another, she had to find a way to get back in her good graces to find out what she knew.

CHAPTER 7
MASK OFF

Coming home from a long day at work, Yvette took off her shoes in the foyer as usual so she wouldn't track the evil spirits of the world into her home. At least that was her spiritual theory. Perhaps it was something she mimicked from another culture. She placed her bare feet down on the cold porcelain and ceramic tile that stretched for what seemed like miles until it met with the plush nylon cream-colored carpeting that covered her living area. The coldness of the ceramic tile underneath her feet felt amazing because they were tired from her working all day.

The corporate VPs were in the market that day, and anyone who's ever worked in the corporate arena knows when the higher-ups are in the market, get ready for the dog and pony show. Usually there are a lot of yes sirs and no sirs and politically correct speaking going on, along with a lot of walking from department to department. Words had to be properly enunciated, and everyone needed to know the numbers and metrics of their department, etc.

Yvette lay sprawled out across her bed in her black pencil skirt and ruffle-breasted short sleeve white top. She wanted to get in a moment of relaxation before she headed to the bathroom to shower. As she rested her eyes, she heard a light tap on the door.

"Yes?" she asked. It was Jaden. He had gotten off work and stood in the doorway with his shirt off and his work pants on.

"Mom, can I use your shower? The nozzle for the hot water broke and I can't get it to turn on."

"What? How did that happen?"

"I don't know, it seems like it's stripped. It just keeps turning around and around but nothing's coming out. As you know, the other full bath upstairs is being remodeled and the half bath downstairs doesn't have a shower. The only option is yours."

"Okay, Jaden, let me take my shower first and then you can take yours."

After graduation, Jaden had taken a summer job until he decided if he wanted to go off to college or not. Yvette hoped that he would decide to get some college experience like his sister, but Jaden steadfastly held to the fact of not going to college. He said it wasn't his thing. Yvette let him know on a regular basis that education is something no one can take from him and that he should strongly consider going to some type of school. She didn't want to push him. He had graduated from high school and at least he was working. Besides, he had recently turned 18. She decided to give him a little time. In the meantime he lived at home with her and Joseph, while Katrina continued her college education three hours away in Austin.

After Yvette finished her shower and got dressed, she called upstairs to Jaden to let him know the shower was free. While he showered, Yvette climbed up into her huge and comfy king-size bed. She grabbed the remote and watched TV on a big 86 inch flat screen. She lay in bed flipping channels wearing a tank top and flannel shorts, her hair pinned in a messy bun. She heard the door chime which was an indicator that someone had opened the door. Joseph was home from work. He walked in and kissed Yvette on the forehead.

"Hey, babe, how was your day?" he asked.

"It was okay," she said. "The corporate VPs were in the market so you know how we had to show up and show out."

"Yeah, I'm sure. I'm going to shower and join you."

"Wait, babe. Jaden is in there taking a shower."

"Why is he taking a shower in our bathroom? There's a bathroom upstairs!" Joseph appeared frustrated and somewhat angry.

"The nozzle broke upstairs on the hot water so he couldn't turn it on. He asked permission and I told him he could take one in ours. What's the problem?" Yvette was confused. She did not understand why Joseph was upset.

"This is our room. He has his space upstairs. There's no reason why he has to shower in here!" Joseph voice elevated.

"So you want him to take a cold shower?"

"Yes! He could have. He's a grown-ass man now. It would not have killed him." And with that Joseph stormed out of the room.

Yvette sat erect in the bed. She was in shock. This side of Joseph continued to rear its ugly head. *He's angry because I allow my child to shower in the bathroom we share,* she thought to herself. Jaden exited the bathroom.

"Thanks, Mom," he said and headed upstairs, unaware of the conversation that transpired between Yvette and Joseph.

Yvette became angry. *How dare he get mad over something so simple? That's my child. I pay bills here, too. Why the fuck can't he shower in any shower in this house no matter where it is?* She fumed while waiting on Joseph to come back so she could tell him how she felt. After about 20 minutes, Jaden came back into the room. He was angry. He stated that Joseph had charged him up about taking a shower in his personal bathroom and that he is to never cross the threshold of the bedroom again. Yvette was livid. She sprang up out of the bed yelling Joseph's name.

"Mom, don't say anything. It's okay. I didn't like the way he approached me. That's all. It's okay."

"No it's not." She walked through the house in pursuit of Joseph and continuously yelled his name. "Joseph! Jaden go upstairs!" she ordered. Jaden did as she demanded. Joseph eventually came in from the backyard patio area.

"Yeah," he answered. The two met up in the dining area of the home.

"What's your problem? You have a problem with him taking a shower in our bathroom?" she stressed. "You can talk to me. I gave him permission!" she yelled.

"You are right … our bathroom!" Joseph rebutted. "He has the entire upstairs. There's no reason for him to be in our space! He towered over Yvette's 5 foot 4 frame. Jaden heard the yelling and saw Joseph inches away from Yvette's face. He immediately jumped between the two. Jaden stood almost as tall as Joseph.

"Man, you better get out of my mom's face!" Jaden yelled aggressively with his eyes locked on Joseph. Like a guard dog he stood in front of his mom. Yvette had never seen this side of Jaden. He was always sweet and calm. Jaden stood toe-to-toe with Joseph and he meant business.

"You better stand down son or … ."

Before he could complete his sentence, Yvette yelled, "Or what? Move Jaden! You're that upset over him taking a goddamn shower! Put your hands on him and you will be sleeping in heavenly peace tonight and I'm not singing a Christmas carol either."

Yvette tried to move Jaden to the side in order to look Joseph in his face to let him know she meant business. She could not budge him. Jaden was still like a guard dog with his eyes fixed and locked on Joseph. His eyes said, "Try me." A few minutes later, Joseph walked away and went into the master bedroom and slammed the door. Yvette was angry. She grabbed her purse, slipped on house shoes and grabbed her car keys.

"Where are you going, Mom?"

"I need to go take a ride and clear my head. I'll be back."

"I'm going with you."

The two of them climbed into the car and Yvette drove off. A few minutes into the drive Yvette begin to sob.

"What's wrong, Mom? Why are you crying?"

"I hate this. I never wanted you to get caught up in the middle of an argument between me and anyone. I never wanted you to feel like you had to protect me," she sobbed. Yvette cried so much she could barely see the road in front of her.

"It's okay, Mom. That's what I'm supposed to do. One of the last things Dad told me after you guys divorced was to make sure I take care of you and my sister. I am." Jaden looked up and realize they were driving through their old neighborhood. Yvette drove up to the house they lived in before she married Joseph and move to their new one. It was almost a year now and the house was still on the market.

She pulled into the driveway and turned the car off. She turned to Jaden and said, "You know, all I ever wanted was for you guys to be happy, right?" She wiped tears from her eyes and continued. "I never want you to feel the need to protect me. This house is still up for sale. We can move back here. I don't want you to ever feel like you're not welcome anywhere I am."

"It's okay, Mom. Maybe he had a bad day. I'm okay." Yvette sat in the driveway of her old home contemplating her life. "Come on, let's go home, Mom, it's getting late." Even though Yvette didn't feel much like it, it was her home at the moment.

She started the car and drove to the house she shared with her husband. They opened the door and there sat Joseph in a single chair in the foyer. He looked despondent. Yvette was still furious that things had gotten heated over a shower. She threw her keys into the glass bowl and walked into the bedroom. Jaden followed suit and started upstairs.

"Hey, man, let me talk to you for a second," Joseph said. Jaden turned around to face Joseph. He stood on the bottom step of the stairway. He stared at Joseph stone-faced. Yvette's ears perked up from the bedroom to hear what Joseph had to say.

"I want to apologize ," he started. "I had a bad day. I was tired and I wanted to take a hot shower and relax. That's all man, I apologize."He extended his hands toward Jaden for a handshake. Jaden was a little reluctant at first but being that his Mom raised him to be God-fearing and to also forgive, he extended his hand and received Joseph's handshake as a peace offering. Then, he retreated upstairs to his room. Now it was time for Joseph to face the music with Yvette. As he headed toward the master bedroom, she came out with a pillow, sheets, comforter, and a blanket.

"Where you going?" he asked.

"I'm sleeping out here on the sofa," she replied.

"Really? Come on, Yvette, don't do this. I'm trying to apologize."

"I don't want to hear it right now, Joseph, since you're so concerned about a fucking shower, you can have the whole room because where my child is not welcome, I will not be!" Yvette continued in a fluster, spreading out the sheets and comforter on a plush tan and chocolate-colored sofa that had numerous plush tan, cream, brown and peach-colored throw pillows. She removed the pillows to create more room for her to lie down.

Joseph pleaded. "Babe I had just come home for work. I wanted to take a shower. I was tired. That's our space! He has the entire three bedrooms upstairs, a game room, and two other bathrooms and a half bath. I rarely go up there. I just want a space that's sacred for us, is that so bad?"

"Look, I know you don't have children so you can't fathom the idea of a bond between a parent and their child, but my children and I are extremely close. They have never not been welcome in any part of a home that I lived in no matter where—especially when I have given them permission. How dare you make him feel unwelcome!"

"It's our room and our space, Yvette!" He threw his hands in the air in frustration.

"Well, take your ass in your room and leave me alone," she said.

"Don't disrespect me like that, Yvette. I'm not cursing at you so don't curse at me."

Yvette lay down on the couch and turned her back to Joseph.

"So, you're really going to sleep out here?"

Yvette did not answer. Joseph went back into the room and slammed the door behind him in defeat. Yvette began to reflect over her life and everything she had been through, once again. She couldn't help but ask to herself, *Did I move too fast, Lord? My desires to be loved, and to be in a meaningful relationship, did I miss something here? Or am I just overreacting?* She wondered again what Elisha had mentioned when they were out the last time. What did she mean by that? She couldn't get it off her mind especially with the recent situations that had occurred between her and Joseph. She had to get to the bottom of that statement and since she and Elisha were not on speaking terms once again, she had to go to the only person that always stayed neutral in their disagreements, Kelsey.

The next morning, Yvette rolled over on the couch, stretched, and opened her eyes to see Joseph standing over her. She was startled.

"What the hell? Why are you standing over me like that?" She pushed herself up to a sitting position on the sofa and wiped her eyes in order to see more clearly.

"I actually just walked in here," Joseph replied. "I was about to wake you to see if you wanted me to cook breakfast or if you wanted to go to breakfast since we are both off today? Listen, I don't want to bring yesterday into today, so let's move past it. Please, Yvette, I love you, okay?"

She stubbornly let it go for the moment and agreed to breakfast at home. During breakfast, Joseph was very catering to her, going above and beyond to get back into her good graces. He cooked an array of different items ranging from French toast, hash browns, scrambled eggs, sliced fruits, turkey bacon and regular bacon. It was topped off by fresh coffee and Mimosas, two of Yvette's favorite breakfast beverages. The food laid across the granite counter tops in individual dishes like a buffet.

"Have a seat, babe." He pulled out a chair for her to sit in. Yvette was still a little disgruntled but she tried not to let it show. She gave a half smile and sat down. With her hair pulled back and wearing a pair of pink and blue yoga pants and a pink tank top, she sat down and sipped on a steaming cup of coffee while Joseph acted like a waiter at IHOP. A few minutes later, Jaden came downstairs on his way to work.

"Hey man," Joseph said, "I made enough breakfast so you can grab something to eat before you go. I even made regular bacon for you because I know you don't like turkey bacon like your mom," he said with a smirk.

"Nah, man, I'm running late, but thanks," Jaden replied. He made eye contact with his mom and said, "I will see you later. I get off at six then I'm going to meet Damian at the gym to shoot some hoops."

"I will see you later," she replied. Breakfast with Joseph was sort of strained. There was still a little tension, mostly on Yvette's side. She managed to let go more and more as breakfast went on and as a few mimosas followed. After all, this was her husband, the man she chose to marry after everything she had been through with the others. *No one is perfect*, she told herself. *We all get upset*, she coaxed herself. She forced conversation and smiles while thinking to herself, *I have to talk to Kelsey. I need her to find out what Elisha knows.* Once breakfast was over, they washed dishes together and cleaned the kitchen.

"You know I was thinking, we have the whole day together. Let's work some of this food off in the bedroom," Joseph said. He grabbed Yvette from behind and kissed her on the neck. Yvette knew she would have to meet up with Kelsey later. She decided to give in to Joseph's invitation for an after breakfast sex romp. She hoped it would make for a smoother exit when she told him she would not be spending the entire day with him, but she would be meeting up with who he considered to be a married mistress. She had to in order to get whatever information possible about him from the bona fide whore, as he referred to her.

Joseph tried to lead her to the bedroom but she stopped to lock the front door just in case Jaden decided to double back. He then turned his attention back to her and looked at her salaciously. Joseph kissed Yvette softly on her neck and undressed her in the kitchen. They never made it into the bedroom.

"You don't want to go into the bedroom?" Yvette asked.

"I'm not quite done eating breakfast yet," he said.

He lifted Yvette off her feet and laid her across the island countertop in their kitchen. The cold granite countertop felt like a block of ice on Yvette's bare back. Joseph took four of Yvette's fluffy oven mitts and placed them under Yvette's head to create a pillow. Yvette's body lay half-way on the countertop with her legs hanging off. Joseph positioned himself between her legs and leaned over to kiss her lips and then her breasts. He reached for a glass that had some leftover mimosa and begin to pour it down Yvette's stomach. Yvette's body tensed up and her back arched as the cold liquid ran over her body and pooled into her navel where Joseph lapped and licked it like a thirsty dog. He got down on his knees and spread Yvette's legs wider as she lay on her back and he poured the remaining mimosa between her legs and drank from her pussy. The coldness of the liquid on her clitoris met the warmth of his tongue and it drove her insane. Just as she started to reach her peak, he stopped. He stood to his feet and draped her legs over his forearms to pull her close to him and inserted himself inside her. He thrust himself back and forth, in and out to climax simultaneously with her. He practically collapsed on top of her and Yvette panted as she tried to gain her composure.

They laid there in the moment. She thought to herself, *damn he primed me real good this time. I didn't even have to think about anyone else.* Even though the act itself didn't last long the priming was all that. He gently slid off her and lifted Yvette from the countertops.

Joseph said, "I was thinking we could catch a movie tonight."

"That sounds like a plan," Yvette said. While everything was feeling euphoric, she also said, "I'm meeting Kelsey for lunch really quick to discuss details for her baby shower."

"Really Yvette?"

"We can't even spend a day together without you having to see her? Damn. Hell she doesn't even know who the baby is for."

"Joseph, that's not your business or your concern. That's my family! How do you know anything about that anyway?" Yvette shouted.

"Don't worry about how I know. I know more than you think."

She gathered her clothes from the floor and angrily stormed into the room.

Feeling regret for his tone and outburst, after some time had passed, Joseph went into the room. "I'm sorry about that," he offered. "I don't want to mess up our morning. Will you at least please be back so that we can get to a 7 o'clock movie? I know how it is when you all get together. You're a happily married woman, they aren't. They are miserable and living lies. I just don't want that spilled over into our marriage," he said.

"Nothing can happen that's not allowed by both of us," Yvette, responded. "Now can you please sterilize the counter? I'm going to shower and I will be back in a couple of hours, long before seven." Yvette patronized Joseph with a kiss and headed to the bathroom to shower.

CHAPTER 8
JOSEPH WHO?

After her shower that morning, Yvette called Kelsey to set up an impromptu lunch since there was never one initially scheduled. "Hey, Kelsey, can you meet me today for lunch? I need to talk to you," Yvette asked.

"Oh Lord! What's wrong?" Kelsey asked.

"Nothing, I need to find out what Elisha meant when she said what she said that day. It's been on my mind and some things have transpired that have me curious."

Kelsey started, "She did share something with me I feel you should know. I really would like her to tell you herself because I don't like giving third-party information besides you two need to squash the bullshit, and secondly, I'm not sure where she's getting this info from. It sounded way too crazy. I damn sure didn't want to repeat it. I'd rather you hear it from the horse's mouth."

"Okay, so where we going to meet?"

"At the spot of course," Kelsey said.

"Damn, Kel! Can't we go somewhere else?"

"We could, but why? It's 10 cents wing Tuesday and I have a cup holder in my car full of dimes and a baby in my belly who loves Club Ignites' daytime wing time Tuesdays."

"Okay, I guess I'll see you there in an hour."

Although Club Ignite was a hot and happening club on Friday and Saturday nights, it also doubled as a great happy hour spot and all-around good place to hang out on certain days leading up to the weekend. Once she arrived, Yvette walked in to find Kelsey already grubbing on some wings.

"Dang! You can't wait for me? You must have gotten here really early," Yvette said.

"Honey child, I was literally down the street getting ready to pass by here when you called. I met up with Raheem and let him feel his baby."

"Girl, you still meeting up with him? I thought you were working on your marriage."

"I am," Kelsey responded. "But he still has to see his baby."

"Kelsey, are you sure this couldn't be Edward's baby, and you're not wanting it to be Raheem's in hopes it will aid in him leaving his live-in baby mama?"

Kelsey stopped and glared at Yvette.

"Okay, forget I said anything!" Yvette said.

Kelsey resumed eating her wings in silence, then said, "We are not here to discuss the paternity of my unborn child. You called me here because you wondered if there's something afoot in la la land where you reside, correct?"

"I guess." Yvette rolled her eyes.

"This is what Elisha mentioned to me. I tried to get her to come to tell you herself, but her exact words were, 'Fuck that wanna-be bougie, fairy tale, dreaming bitch. Let her bump her fucking head once more.'"

"Oh, really? She's talking like she thinks she knows some factual shit."

"She said she went to a reggae club one night called the Dew Drop to meet up with this young Rasta she met at a red light while driving and exchanged numbers with. She said they were off in the cut towards the back of the club, ducked off where they could see everything and everyone, and in walks your husband."

"My husband?"

"Yes, your husband."

"That is weird. Joseph claims he hates clubs and never mentioned going to any club. He always acts like he's so busy at work and can't wait to get home and rest."

"She said she just watched him for a few minutes to see if he was meeting with a chick, but he was at the bar hanging out and having a few drinks with some guys. She also said after a little while, she decided to leave, but the exit door was right by the bar and she had to pass by Joseph to get out. She decided to go for it anyway and held her purse up to cover her face as she passed by. Apparently Joseph was caught up in his conversation. He didn't even notice her, but one thing she said she noticed is that he was having a full-blown conversation with the guys in Patois and they referred to him by another name. She said they kept calling him what sounded like Steven but their accents was so heavy, she wasn't sure. But on her way out, another guy walked in and called him by that name again."

Yvette sat there in silence and stared off totally zoned out. She reflected on the conversation she overheard a few nights ago while Joseph was on the patio. "Yvette, Yvette, snap out of it, girl! I'm not sure how factual this is. I'm just telling you what she said to me. Has Joseph ever mentioned anything about being from Jamaica or having family in Jamaica?"

"No, and that bitch probably was drunk and don't know what she heard."

"Girl, why would she repeat something like that if she wasn't sure?"

"I'll tell you why, because she's a miserable bitch, that's why. Girl, I got to go!" Yvette gathered her keys and purse to leave.

"How in the hell are you going to ask me to meet you here because you wanted to talk and then leave not even eating anything or drinking anything just because you didn't like what you heard?"

"Kelsey. You said you were down the street anyway so what does it matter?"

"That's exactly why you and Elisha can't see eye-to-eye. You only think of yourself. We have been there for you time and time again and for what? Soon as you hear something you don't like, you are ready to bolt. Well, guess what? I'm done eating anyway! Next time you want to talk, don't call me!" Kelsey got up from the table to exit but not before leaving Yvette with some parting words. "You try so hard to create the perfect life, but you continue to make fucked up choices. Have it ever dawned on you or did you ever ask yourself why he only had friends and work associates at the wedding? Start listening to your gut and not your heart, or for that matter satisfying what's between your legs. I'm aware of the big mess I'm in, and Elisha is aware of her mess. Protect your shit if that's what you want to do, but don't act like everyone is out to destroy you or lie to you because that's what you're used to!"

Kelsey then left abruptly before Yvette could make it to the door. Yvette's mind was reeling. She knew some of what Kelsey said Elisha told her was true, but being called by another name than Joseph? *What the fuck?* Yvette also pondered the reason there were not any of Joseph's family members at the wedding. He said his mom was ill with Alzheimer's and he was an only child, but not one family member? Yvette's ride home felt like the longest ride ever. She thought about how she had a tendency to always move too fast and how she wanted to believe in love so badly. This newfound information was mind-blowing, yet she didn't quite know what she was going to do with it. She wasn't ready to confront Joseph, nor did she want to give way to another break up and failed marriage. Lately, Joseph had exhibited a bit of controlling behavior, especially now that they were married. He was such a gentleman before. *Does marriage really change people?* she thought.

She pulled into the driveway. Joseph's car was still there as if it never moved. Yvette exited her vehicle and entered the house to find Joseph lying across the bed watching a game.

"Hey, babe," he said. "How did the baby shower planning go?"

"What?" she replied.

"Didn't you meet up with Kelsey to discuss the baby shower?" he asked suspiciously.

"Oh yeah, right. I'm just in deep thought about work. I got a call that we will have another corporate visit on Monday. I was thinking about what I need to do to make sure I'm prepared," she said.

She quickly thought about something to explain her lack of response about the baby shower planning that was supposed to be the reason she and Kelsey met for lunch.

"So what do you want to do tonight?" Joseph asked. "Dinner, a movie or both?"

"I was really thinking we could stay in. I really don't feel like getting dressed to go out anywhere. Besides I need to jot down some notes for the visit."

Before Joseph could rebut her, Yvette's phone rang. It was her mother.

"Hey, Mom, how are you?"

She answered, "Oh, I'm fine, I was calling to ask you if everything was okay with Katrina?"

"As far as I know it is. Why do you ask?"

"I have been looking at her Facebook page and every now and again she posts something about depression. Have you talked with her?"

"Not since last weekend. I try to give her space since she's in college."

"I wish you wouldn't have sent her so far away from home to school. I don't think she was ready."

"Mom, she's fine. She has to learn to adapt. She's 21 years old, now."

"And what does that mean?" Yvette's mom asked abruptly.

"Look, Mom, I will call and talk to her okay?"

"Yvette, I know you're practically newly-married but I really wish you would have taken some time out to make sure these children were okay with all of the transition, the situation with Geo and the gun play, now this marriage. How much did you really know about this man before you married? I've only chatted on the phone with him and I only saw him at the wedding due to distance and something just didn't sit well with me. Where was his people, did he not have any family there, Yvette?"

"Mom!" Yvette said and walked out of the bedroom and into the backyard patio and closed the door behind her. "His mom was ill at the time and couldn't make it. I told you that."

"I understand that but no one else, not an uncle, cousin, or aunt?"

"He says he's not that close with the rest of his family."

"Why are you asking me all this now? We got married almost a year ago."

"I didn't want to rain on your happiness. You seem to have come out of that dark place you were in and I didn't want to see you there ever again. Look, just please check on Katrina. You know most people that go through depression will never say they are depressed when asked. Just be mindful of that."

"Okay, Mom. I will check on her."

"Thank you, and I love you, Yvette. Continue to watch and pay attention to those children. Although they're older, they still need you."

"I know that, Mom."

"Okay, okay, I will leave it alone. I will talk to you, later. I love you."

"I love you, too, Mom."

Yvette returned to the bedroom to find Joseph looking at her in an obscure manner.

"Why are you looking at me like that?" she asked.

"Since when do you have to leave the room to talk to your mom?" he asked.

"Since I wanted to have a personal conversation with my mom that did not include you. Is that a problem?"

Joseph grabbed the remote, fluffed his pillow, and leaned back against the headboard of the bed with nothing more to say. He flipped through the TV channels. Yvette removed herself from the situation and went into the living area to make a call to Katrina. She situated herself on the sofa, and looked around at the high cathedral ceilings and enormous bay windows adorned throughout. The sunlight shined through them. She pulled her feet up on the sofa and folded her legs behind her and begin to dial Katrina's number.

"Hi, Mom," Katrina answered.

"Hey, love, how are you?"

"I'm okay," she answered. "Your grandmother doesn't seem to think so. She says you're posting things about depression on your page."

"Oh, it's just to raise awareness."

"Are you sure? You know you can talk to me if you need to Katrina."

"Yes, Mom, I know. I do wish I could have my dorm room to myself. My roommate keeps inviting people over and playing loud music. They stay over late and I end up having to go to the common area to study all the time."

"Oh hell no! I need to make a trip up there!" Yvette yelled.

"No, Mom, I will handle it. You can't always come to bail me out."

"You know you can always come home and go to school here."

"I'm fine, Mom. I got to go though, I need to get to work. I will call you later in the week."

"Okay Katrina. I love you."

"I love you, too, Mom."

Yvette hung up the phone with a helpless feeling. She was known to go to bat for her children, make phone calls, and show up on their behalf, but she couldn't do that anymore.

She had to let them grow up and learn to fight their own battles, which was extremely hard for her to accept. She sat on the sofa and felt defeated. She reflected over the day's episodes, the information she heard from Kelsey, and her mom's concerns about her husband which tied into the information she received. Her biggest concern was Katrina possibly crying out indirectly about depression. Yvette let out a deep sigh and laid down on the sofa. Around midnight, she heard someone calling her name in a soft whisper. She opened her eyes to find Joseph standing over her. She had apparently fallen asleep on the sofa and he had fallen asleep in the bed. He woke up and noticed she wasn't there. He went to look for her.

"Come to bed," he said. Yvette focused her eyes and tried to get steady on her feet. She toggled along behind him into the bedroom.

The next morning, the two awakened and prepared to head out for work. Before Joseph left out of the door, he kissed her on the lips and said, "Good luck with your corporate visit today."

"Huh?" Yvette replied. She was puzzled. She had forgotten she lied about why her mind had been preoccupied after her visit with Kelsey.

"Your corporate visit. That you're having again today."

"Oh yeah, right, thanks." Joseph gave her a strange look once again and headed out of the door.

While at work, she couldn't seem to focus at all. Her mind was clouded.

"Hey girl, snap out of it. You are in deep thought. What's going on?" asked her co-worker, Mia. She was Yvette's work bestie. They never really hung out away from work. They did have lunch together and cut up in the office though. Mia was slender and tall about 5 foot 9, but when she put on her heels, she was damn near six foot two. She was a gorgeous coppertone woman with beautiful skin. She kept her hair laid and her makeup was always flawless.

"Girl, I got a lot on my mind," Yvette responded.

"Spill it," Mia urged her. "It's always better out than in or is that what they usually say when someone has gas?" she chuckled slightly.

"Girl, you're crazy. For starters, I'm concerned about my daughter, Katrina. She seems to have trouble with her roommate and I'm trying to let her handle it on her own. To top it off, my mom seems to think she may be going through some sort of depression."

"Girl, do we need to roll up there? Because you know we look as young as they do or they look as old as us. Either way, we can go whoop some ass. What's good?" Mia was poised and professional but was a nice mixture of Kelsey and Elisha when need be. "I'm just saying, friend, we can roll up there with hoodies on, beat that bitch ass, and roll out in the dark of night. We are three and a half hours away who's going to know?"

"While I admire your plan, because I was thinking of something similar, I have to give her room to fight her own battles."

"Okay, just know that I'm down for the cause."

Yvette changed the subject. She remembered something about Mia. "Hey, Mia, whatever happened on your second date with the guy you said you and your sister met at the spot a few weeks ago? Didn't you go out with him again this weekend?"

"Yes, I actually did. Girl! Why this brother was missing a front tooth?"

"What?" Yvette laughed. "You didn't see that the night you met him?"

"You know it was dark. He was tall, big, and burly, just like I like them and I was full of that ish," Mia responded. "I blame it on my sister though even though she said she tried to tell me."

"What are you going to do?"

"Hey, I don't know. I most definitely can't take him around my friends."

"Is he a nice guy though," Yvette questioned,

"Because you know that can be fixed, right?"

"He is missing a freaking tooth and he's a grown-ass man. He knows its missing and he has a good job, why hasn't he fixed it before now?"

"Maybe he has a dentist phobia," Yvette said.

"Good day, I'm going back to my office." Mia walked away and mumbled, "He's a grown-ass man. I will see you at lunch, girl." Yvette laughed.

While at her desk, she thought, *I have to find a way to talk to Elisha for myself and find out what she knows.*

CHAPTER 9
TRYING TO CONTROL THE UNCONTROLLABLE

A few days later during the weekend, Yvette thought it would be a great idea to try to reach out to Kelsey to see if they could set up a "come to Jesus" meeting with Elisha to find out what she knows about Joseph. She called Kelsey.

"Hey, chick."

"Hey, Vet. What's going on?" They would sometimes shorten each other's full name to a nickname.

"I have been thinking about what you said that Elisha knows and I really need to talk to her."

"Why bother? All is well, right? I wouldn't concern myself with that. You know how she is." Yvette got quiet for a minute. "All is well, right?"

"There is something that I'm not sure of. I'm not going to elaborate on right now. I want to see what else she knows."

"You know she not messing with you anymore at all. How are you supposed to do that?"

"I was hoping you…."

"Oh, hell, no," Kelsey interrupted. "I'm not getting involved. I tried that last time and you messed it up with your arrogance. No ma'am!"

"Me? Arrogant? I was just … okay, never mind."

"Why don't you call her, yourself?"

"I tried. I think she has my number blocked."

"So this stuff that you can't elaborate on, is it serious?"

"Yes, it might cost me my marriage." There was a dead silence on the phone. Kelsey didn't ask any more questions.

"Okay, I will set it up again like before. This time, please be humble."

"I'm always humble."

"Really, Yvette."

"Okay, okay I will be more humble."

After hanging up with Yvette, Kelsey gave Elisha a call.

"Hey, girl, long time no hear. What's going on with you over there? Honeymooning again with your husband? You haven't called anybody," Kelsey said.

"Bitch, honeymooning? Yeah right. I just been doing me besides your big ass is pregnant and I don't fuck with Miss wannabe Sadity Kitty Yvette."

"Don't be like that, anyway you know I'm prego and hungry. Let's go get something to eat. We haven't hung out in a minute."

"Bitch, where you trying to go, because my money is funny right now. I've been hanging out too much and I have to recoup my spending."

Kelsey said, "That's okay, I got you."

"Child I'm always down for some free food! By the way, bitch did you ever find out who that baby for?"

"Girl! I already told you it's for Raheem."

"And you back with your husband and he doesn't know. Biiiiiittttccchh! Where are we going because I'm going to need a drink."

The pair decided to meet up at Los Cucos Mexican Cafe and have a margarita and some Mexican food. They met up in the parking lot and the two walked in, found a table and the waitress came over and took their orders. She brought back two margaritas, one frozen and the other on the rocks with no alcohol.

Elisha laughed," Girl, that's a waste of a margarita if you can't have alcohol."

"I'm just going to pretend," Kelsey responded.

"You keep pretending bitch. In the meantime I will have that shot of tequila that was meant to be in yours, in mine!"

Elisha noticed that Kelsey constantly looked at her phone and replied to a text.

"You must be making plans to meet up with your potential baby daddy afterwards, by the way you keep texting and checking your phone," Elisha stated.

"Excuse you? Potential?"

"Bitch I need you to get really real about the possibilities that this might be your husband's baby and not Raheem's."

"Elisha, shut up, shit! You would try to ruin a wet dream if you could."

Exploding with laughter, Elisha said, "Y'all have such a hard time dealing with me because I keep it real and say the shit y'all want to say."

"Elisha, everything you want to say doesn't always have to be said."

"Ummmm, yes it does. Some people live in a place of denial and they like to dwell there and then they invite their neighbors over who also dwell in Denialville and they have little denial gatherings and conversations with each other and support the denial that they are in, all the while being content. I am what you would call the denial burglar. I come to steal all denial and put you on game! Shit! Stop playing with yourself, Kelsey, seriously though."

Kelsey looked at Elisha who looked convinced and unwavering in her statement. Kelsey burst out in laughter.

"You are so damn stupid! Really? Denial burglar?"

"Yes, bitch, I'm snatching all doubt, denial, all that shit." She gestured back and forth with her hands as if she were snatching something. The two of them laughed hysterically. Yvette walked up to the table and the laughter immediately stopped. Elisha looked as if she saw a ghost and Kelsey looked like the cat that swallowed the canary.

"Hey, Elisha," Yvette started.

Elisha looked over at Kelsey and said, "Really bitch? Really? You trying that Kumbaya shit again?"

"Elisha come on. It has been a long time. We are family and she wants to get past this."

"I don't have shit to say," Elisha stated firmly.

"Look, Elisha, I know I come off wrong sometimes but we have been like the Three Musketeers," Yvette said.

"Yeah we were, until you got remarried and thought you were better and forgot your own bone closet you needed to clear out."

Yvette took a deep breath because her ultimate goal was to find out more about what Elisha knew. She suppressed how she really wanted to respond and manage to utter the words, "You're right."

"Say what now?"

"You're right?"

"I'm what?" Elisha mocked her by holding her hand to her ear. She urged Yvette to repeat what she said again. "Say it louder for the people in the back!" she taunted.

Yvette repeated it louder. "I said you're right!"

Elisha face softened and the look of disdain and anger disappeared as though she had been waiting to hear those words for a long time. A slight smile came across her face.

"Sit down, bitch. You standing up there like you about to take our order."

Yvette breathed a sigh of relief and sat down as the three of them laughed simultaneously at Elisha's antics. As the day turned into night, the threesome found themselves laughing and catching up like old times.

"So, how's the marriage going, Yvette?" Elisha asked sarcastically. Elisha sipped a margarita and stared at her while she waited for Yvette to respond.

"If you must know, I'm adjusting. Some days are great and some days I think to myself *what have I done?* I was home free, out of my first marriage—just me and my two. Free to roam and live my life on my own terms," Yvette reflected.

"I tell you what, if I decide to get a divorce, I will never marry again," Elisha stated.

Kelsey cleared her throat. She tried to signal to Yvette that it was the perfect time to ask Elisha about what she knew that pertained to Joseph. Yvette didn't catch on at first, so she did it once more.

"Bitch take a sip of that fake-ass margarita you've been sipping on. Is the baby giving you itchy throat? I've heard of heartburn but damn!" Elisha said.

Yvette finally caught on. "Lisha you know," Yvette started.

"Awww, hell you shortening my name. What the fuck is up?"

"No, seriously, something has transpired with Joseph and I was just wondering about what you mentioned last time."

"So, that's it huh?" Elisha said. "That's the only fucking reason you're here. Not because you're sincere about what you said, but because you wanted some info. Typical Yvette, always about self." Elisha grabbed her purse and started to leave.

"Elisha!" Kelsey shouted. "Don't leave like that."

"You shut up. You knew about this. That's why you sounded like a cat choking on a hairball earlier and you were constantly texting. That's what that was all about!"

"I'm sorry," Yvette shouted.

Elisha stopped in her tracks.

Yvette continued, "I'm sorry that I pretend like my shit don't stink, and that I'm a goody two-shoes. What I do know is that we are family and moreover we're friends. Elisha I would never knowingly hold information from you that could be detrimental to you."

Elisha turned around with a scowl on her face. "You live in the same town as this bitch, Denialville. Why should I say anything? So I can get accused of wanting you to be miserable again like me?"

"Come on, Elisha," Kelsey pleaded.

"Please?" Yvette asked. Both of them looked at Elisha.

There was a long pause before Elisha finally said, "Stop sitting there looking like two pitiful ass pound puppies. She walked back to the table and threw her purse down on the table top. She sat back in her chair with her arms folded. "What I meant by what I said the last time, that you should have looked deep before you leaped, was because I found out Joseph is from Jamaica. I hang out at this club where mostly people from the Caribbean hang out. Prior to me seeing him there with my own eyes, I was told that by a chick who used to date him. I don't like believing everything I hear but when I saw him there and I've heard him speaking Patois, I knew she wasn't lying."

"What!" Kelsey shouted. "Why would he not say that?"

"According to the chick I met who dated him, his mom still lives there and prefers for him to be with Jamaican women over American women."

"He told me his mom was from South Carolina and she was ill with Alzheimer's and that's why she couldn't make it to the wedding. He also said his father was dead."

Yvette was confused for a moment, then her phone rang. It was Katrina but she sent it to voicemail with the intent to call her back when she finished getting the tea about what Elisha knew.

"Honey, this chick said that Joseph's mom and dad are alive and well and he also has a sister. They all live in Kingston, Jamaica. Joseph went to high school and college here. He lived with friends of the family who relocated here with their son who was best friends with Joseph. This is probably why he doesn't have much of an accent. They wanted him to have a better educational opportunity according to what she said he told her. She said they broke up, rather she broke up with him because he kept reminding her that his mom really wanted him to marry an island girl and not an American girl. She grew exhausted of that and his on-and-off-again, temper. She also mentioned some other things but that's irrelevant."

"Why would you say that and then tell me it's irrelevant?" Yvette asked.

"Girl, you know how some females get when they stop messing with a guy all of a sudden. His sex was wack, he was a two-minute brother all that bullshit, but according to her, they were together two years. *Bitch what? All that and you and you stayed for two years?* is what I said to myself when she told me all of this."

Yvette looked down in disbelief and shame. Some part of her felt Elisha found some type of victory in knowing this and telling her. It was almost like, bitch you thought you found yourself a prince now what? He's still a frog. Part of her wanted to cry, another part was angry, and still another part felt stupid. Why did he have to lie? She didn't know how to feel.

"It's okay, Yvette. We are all dealing with some type of shit in our marriage. If you choose to work through this, it's okay," Kelsey reassured her with her hand on Yvette's shoulder. Yvette's phone rang. It was Katrina again. She decided to answer.

"Hey, baby girl, what's up? It's 11 pm, why are you still awake? Don't you have class early in the morning?"

There was no response at first, then she heard Katrina say, "Mom." But it sounded more like a moan. It dragged on.

"What's wrong!" Yvette shouted.

Katrina's only response was "Mom" in the same moaning sound.

"Something is wrong with Katrina!" Yvette shouted. "I got to get to Austin. She sounds like she's drunk, drugged, or in pain. She won't say anything other than 'Mom.'" Yvette frantically gathered her purse and keys from the table.

"Wait I'm driving," Elisha said. "You can't drive like this."

"I'm going, too," Kelsey said. "Yvette, you stay on the phone and keep talking to her. I'm going to call the police and the paramedics and get them to her dorm."

A million things ran through Yvette's mind as she tried to remain composed. She kept calling her daughter's name. "Paramedics and police are on the way," Kelsey said.

About 10 minutes went by while Kelsey coordinated the first responders in Austin … and that felt like 10 days with Yvette holding the phone listening to her daughter breathe and moan. Elisha drove reckless at what seemed like warp speed shouting, "Get the fuck out of the way stupid ass mother fuckers!" the entire way.

"You're going to be okay," Yvette said as she tried to comfort Katrina. She then began to pray. She heard a voice on the other end of the line.

"Mrs. Jennings? This is Officer Cannon with Austin PD. We have the medics here."

"What's going on? What are the paramedics saying? What's wrong with my daughter?"

"It appears that your daughter has suffered from an overdose on over-the-counter medications. They are going to get her over to the hospital. You can meet us there. They will pump her stomach so drive safely. She's going to be okay. We don't want to have to send an ambulance for you, okay?" Yvette became quiet. She was in disbelief. "Mrs. Jennings do you hear me?"

"Yes, officer, I hear you." Yvette hung up the phone and let out a cry that would frighten a screaming banshee. "Why?" she asked. "What am I doing wrong?" She sobbed inconsolably.

The drive seemed to take forever. Nothing but silence surrounded the sounds of Yvette's sniffles. Three and a half hours went by and they finally arrived at Austin General Hospital. Yvette bolted from the car and left the door open. The other two ran behind her. It was almost 2:30 am by the time they arrived. Yvette's phone had been blowing up with calls from Joseph that went unanswered who was back home losing his mind. Yvette didn't care with her recent findings. Katrina was her only concern—no one and nothing else mattered. The three rushed into the doors of the emergency room and made their way to the nurse's station.

"My daughter, Katrina, was brought here probably three hours or so ago."

"Are you Miss Yvette Jennings?" the nurse asked.

"Yes I am," Yvette replied.

"I will go get the doctor for you. Wait here." A few minutes went by and the doctor came to the area where Kelsey, Yvette, and Elisha waited.

"Mrs. Jennings?"

"Yes, call me Yvette."

"I'm Dr. Jones. I will take you back to see your daughter, I have a few things I wanted to ask and let you know. Is your daughter into any drugs or does she suffer from depression, lately?"

"Drugs? No, never. She's a good girl. Depression? I don't think so. I know she was having a few problems at school other than that, I wasn't aware of anything else."

"We have been trying to get her to tell us what she had taken, but she keeps saying nothing. We have pumped her stomach, but as a reaction to whatever she has taken, she is having seizures on and off. Unless we find out what she took we can't effectively treat it. We may have to do a spinal tap."

"I will get her to talk, doctor. She is probably embarrassed."

The doctor led her to the room. The other ladies stayed behind in the waiting area. Katrina lay on her back staring at the ceiling.

"Hey, hunny, bunny," Yvette said. "How are you feeling?"

"I'm okay," Katrina replied.

"Why did you do this?"

"I was overwhelmed in school, my roommate was harassing me, you were busy with work and your new husband. I tried to cope the best I could, and when I couldn't, part of me wanted to die. Things changed so much when you got married, Mom. It had just been us—me, you, and Jaden. Then, there was school, your new husband, everything!"

"Katrina, you're going to have to tell the doctors what you took so that they can treat you. Otherwise they're going to have to stick a big needle in your back."

Katrina became quiet and her eyes rolled into the back of her head and she began to convulse and shake violently. She was having another seizure. Yvette put her hand on Katrina's chest as though she was trying to keep her still. She didn't want her to fall out of the hospital bed.

"Nurse!" she called out loudly. They were already on the way and burst through the door. Yvette was in hysterics. She didn't know what to do. She could only stand there helplessly, watch the action in front of her, and cry. Once the seizure subsided, Yvette pleaded once again with her daughter to tell the doctor what she had taken. Katrina finally told them the mixture of over the counter meds, consisting of Tylenol PM, Aspirin, and other pain medicine. They were able to ultimately diagnose and start treatment that would stop the seizures. Meanwhile Joseph called Katrina's and Elisha's phones back to back. They were on pins and needles in the waiting area. Elisha finally decided to answer.

"Hello? Hey it's Joseph. I know it's late but have you seen Yvette?" he asked.

"Joseph, I was trying to wait and let her call you and tell you herself, but we are in Austin."

"Austin!" Joseph shouted before she could finish. "What the hell are y'all doing in Austin?"

"Yvette does have a child here or did you forget?" Elisha replied smugly.

"Look I don't have time for this. It's 3 am and I have been calling all night and half of the morning. What's going on?" he asked.

"Something happened with Katrina and we are here at the hospital."

"What? Why wouldn't she call me first? Why the hell would she call y'all? I'm her husband."

"Look, Negro! We just happened to all be together when she got the call. Okay?"

"That's the problem right there. I have been calling all night over 50 times and y'all couldn't pick up."

"Look, your own wife didn't pick up. Who the fuck are we to answer if she doesn't?" Elisha barked back.

Kelsey interrupted, "Tell him I'm going to get Yvette to call him back as soon as we find out what's going on and stop arguing with that man," she said aggressively. "This is not the time or the place for that."

"Okay," Elisha said and hung up the phone without saying anything further.

"Why you hang up in the man face like that?" Kelsey asked.

"Because I don't like him, that's why."

"You thought he was amazing and such a great catch before."

"That's before I found out he was a fucking liar like all the rest." Yvette appeared back in the waiting area and the two ladies jumped to their feet.

"Is she okay, Yvette? What's going on?" Kelsey asked.

"She's better now," Yvette replied. They have pumped her stomach and she finally told them everything she took so they were able to work on getting the seizures to stop. She's resting now. Once they release her in the morning I'm going to rent a truck, pack her things and transfer her back home."

"Can we get a room and get some rest for a few hours? We will stay and help you, but in the meantime call your husband. He has been blowing us up," Kelsey said.

"And there's that," Yvette said. "Thank you both for coming with me. I appreciate it."

"That's what we do," Elisha said.

"Let me go deal with this," Yvette said and walked out of the ER doors in order to have a private conversation with Joseph. The other two stayed behind and got snacks out of the hospital's vending machine to try and nourish their early morning munchies. As they looked through the hospital's glass doors they could see Yvette and she appeared to be yelling, judging by her facial expressions and hand movements. A few minutes later she returned inside.

"You okay, girl?" Kelsey asked.

"Yeah, I'm fine. I was, trying to tell him what's going on, and all he could talk about is the fact that I drove all the way here and didn't tell him I was with y'all. He said I wouldn't answer but Elisha had to be the one to take his call."

"He kept calling my fucking phone! He should be glad I answered!"

"Yvette, you didn't mention anything to him about what Elisha told you yet, did you?" Kelsey asked.

"No that's a conversation we are going to have face-to-face," she responded.

Let's get a hotel and grab something to eat. Kelsey I know you're tired and hungry, eating for two. I bet you're starved."

With a bag of Cheetos in one hand and a Snickers bar in the other, she replied, "I am, but I was going to make this candy bar and bag of chips do what it do."

The three managed a laugh and proceeded to the car to find food and a place to sleep for a while. After getting Katrina released from the hospital and putting in a transfer at the college, Yvette rented a truck big enough to pack up all of Katrina's belongings then started the trip back to Dallas with Kelsey and Elisha following behind in her car.

CHAPTER 10
STRANGER DANGER

The drive home seem like an eternity. Yvette finally pulled into the driveway. She thanked Elisha and Kelsey once more and told them to take her car to their house and she would communicate with them later in the day to retrieve it. Yvette left everything in the truck. She just wanted to get Katrina settled, shower, and get some sleep.

"I'm sorry about everything, Mom. I don't know what I was thinking," Katrina said somberly.

"Let's not talk about that right now. Go upstairs and get some rest," Yvette said. Katrina turned to go upstairs and her mother said, "Promise me that no matter what you're feeling next time, if you're lost, in despair or confused, promise me you will call me no matter what. I don't care how big or small the issue may be, it's not a bother. You are my child so don't ever feel that way no matter how old you are or how far away you may be. I apologize if I were not there for you or I made you feel otherwise." She used her index finger to lift Katrina's face so that she looked her in her eyes. "I love you, okay?"

"I love you, too, Mom." She gave her mom a hug and went upstairs. Yvette took a deep sigh and began peeling off her clothing en route to the master bedroom. She expected to find Joseph there, but she looked around the room, puzzled. *Now I know I saw his car parked outside. Maybe he's out with a friend and he picked them up in their vehicle,* she thought. She didn't think any more of it. She went ahead and showered. The hot steamy water beat down all over her body. It was exactly what she needed. While in the shower, she began to think over her life and all of the mistakes she made as she tried to find love. This marriage could be another possible mistake. She also thought about the missed opportunities with her daughter, things that went unnoticed because she was caught up in her own needs and desires. Tears began to stream down her face. *Why do I keep doing this?* she asked herself. *Why do I keep putting myself through this?* She then began to sob.

After a good cry and a hot shower, she felt a tad bit better. She exited the shower and expected that her husband would be possibly there. He wasn't. However, she heard the faint sound of conversation in a distance once again. Clothed in her purple fuzzy robe, trendells of her hair hung down in her face and down her neck after it fell out of the clamp that she used to pin it up while showering. She made her way down the marble floored hallway and onto the carpet of the living area in her bare feet. Lo and behold, on the patio Joseph was on the phone, speaking to someone in Patois. He was so engaged in conversation that he hadn't even realized she had made it home. Yvette was careful and quiet. She didn't want him to know she was listening. When he seemed to be wrapping up the conversation, she scurried off back into the bedroom. She appeared like she had just come out of the bathroom. Joseph seemed surprised when he saw her. He stood in the middle of their bedroom wearing a white wife beater tank top and gray sweatpants. His dreads hung over his broad shoulders. He stood there with a sheepish look.

"Hey, babe, when did you get in?" he asked.

"Obviously long enough ago to clean up. I didn't see you in the house anywhere. I was tired and went ahead and showered," she replied. She abruptly stared at him and anticipated the forthcoming lies.

"Wow, what's with the attitude? I should be the one who's upset. You go to Austin because something happened with Katrina and you didn't even bother to call me and on top of that you ignore my calls the whole time. I had to hear from that whoring-ass cousin about where you were and what was going on!"

"Hold on, don't call her out of her name, Joseph."

"I just called them like I see them," he replied. Yvette grew angrier by the minute. *How dare his lying ass have the audacity to call anybody anything other than their name?* she thought.

"Where were you when I got home?" Yvette asked.

"What do you mean where was I? I was here."

"Yeah but I didn't see you anywhere."

"Had you bothered to check the backyard you would have seen me. I was in the back straightening up a few things. Is that a problem?"

"Straightening up a few things, huh?"

"Yeah, the water hose wasn't where it should have been. I watered a few of the plants. Look, I don't know what you're on right now but I'm the one who should be pissed."

Joseph stormed off into the bathroom and slammed the door. Yvette noticed that he left his phone behind. She picked up the phone and checked the call log to see the last number he had dialed or had called him. The area code of

the last incoming call was one she had never seen before. It
started with 876. She was tempted to hit the redial button.
She wanted to hear the voice on the other end. She wanted
to know who he was talking to and why he was hiding it.
Curiosity took over, and she gave way to it. Yvette hit the
redial button on the phone and the phone rang and rang.
She was about to hang up when a woman answered. She
sounded like she was aged but she had a distinctive and
heavy accent.

"Hello, son," she answered. Yvette didn't say anything.
"Steven," the woman on the other line called out, "My son,
why are you not answering me?"

Yvette was in a state of shock. She stood there and held
the phone in a trance. Joseph walked out of the bathroom
and saw her with his phone in her hand. He could hear his
mother's voice coming through the receiver. He figured she
now knew it was his mother in Jamaica on the other end.

"What are you doing with my phone!" he shouted. He
snatched his phone from Yvette and went out onto the patio
to converse with his mother. She was clueless concerning
what was going on. Yvette listened to him speak to his
mother in his native tongue, while she peered through the
glass sliding door with her arms folded firmly. She was
angry. As Joseph wrapped up his conversation, Yvette
flipped the lock button on the patio door and locked him
outside.

"Open the door," Yvette!" he demanded.

"Open the door for whom? Who the fuck are you? The
man I married is named Joseph! You're a fucking stranger. I
don't know a Steven," she shouted through the glass door.

"Let me in and I can explain."

"Explain from outside. I can hear you!"

"Yvette, come on man, these mosquitoes are biting me."

"I don't care. Go on and straighten up the yard like you lied and said you were doing earlier. I heard you on the phone and this is not the first time! You're a liar. I don't know who you are. You are a damn stranger!"

"Stop calling me that," he yelled. "Open the door. You got me out here yelling. The neighbors are going to come out and these mosquitoes are eating me up." Joseph banged on the door and grew increasingly and noticeably angry. "Okay!" he yelled. "I'm originally from Jamaica so are my parents. I have one sister. I came here when I was 12 for a better education with a family friend. I lied because my mother and family do not want me taking up with an American woman. My parents don't know we're married and I'm trying to find a way to tell them!"

Yvette's mouth dropped wide open. *My whole marriage is a lie* she thought. "Everything you said I already knew. I only wanted to hear it from your mouth. Yeah, I heard about the woman you dated before me and how she broke up with you for that bullshit. I also know about you going to the Caribbean Club on Hanson Street. Yeah, Elisha, told me she saw you there. You were so caught up speaking Patois with the natives you didn't even see her. Guess what? She saw your ass!"

"Elisha? Fuck that bitch. She has tried to fuck every nigga in there but nobody wants her ass, not even her own damn husband. Open the door, Yvette!"

Joseph's voice changed and so did the look in his eyes. Yvette became frightened. She knew she couldn't leave him out there all night. She stood there for a minute then slowly slid the latch back to unlock the door. She braced herself for what was to come. She stepped back and allowed him to come in. He was pissed and he scratched areas on his arms where he had been bitten.

"That's the problem in our marriage now. You let outside interference infiltrate our marriage."

"Outside interference!" she shouted. "I don't even know who the fuck you are!"

"Stop cursing at me like that. You've been hanging around them and that's how you talk to me now!"

He gave her that look again and used the same tone that frightened her earlier. It gave her pause. Yvette said nothing more. She stood there and glared at him.

"Now I got to go find some ointment or alcohol to put on these damn mosquito bites."

Joseph went into the bathroom in the master bedroom. Yvette sat on the sofa and thought about her next move, now that she knew the truth. She could hear Joseph turn on the TV. He then turned off the light and climbed into bed without saying anything more on the subject. Yvette was at a loss for words. She decided she was not going to sleep in the bed with him that night. She retrieved some spare bedding from the hall closet, made up the couch as comfortable as she could, and settled down to sleep. She couldn't. Many questions swirled in her mind. There were many what-ifs and whys. She cried once more. She cried so much her pillow became soaked.

As the night passed, she managed to fall asleep. The living room was almost pitch dark and only bits of light shined in from the night sky. Yvette tossed and turned, trying to get comfortable. Upon finally getting comfortable, she closed her eyes tightly and doze off again. She laid on her back with her arms resting on her chest. She felt a presence over her. Yvette opened her eyes to find Joseph inches away from her face. He glared at her. It startled her and she began to flail her arms and swing in the dark. She slapped Joseph in the face. That angered him and he aggressively grabbed her wrist and scratched her in the process. Her wrist began to bleed slightly.

"Why were you standing over me in the dark?" she said and snatched her wrist from his grip. She sat up fully and turned on the lamp near the sofa in order to see.

"So you're sleeping on the sofa again now, really?" he stated angrily.

"I need some space away from you to process all of this. So yes, I am," she responded.

"No wife of mine will reside with me and sleep on the couch when she should be in bed with me."

"Me being your wife is up for debate right now, being as though I married Joseph and your real name is Steven."

"There is no debate. Come to bed," he demanded.

"Boy, bye. I said I'm going to sleep here and clear my head tonight so goodnight!" Yvette then turned off the lamp, turned her back to Joseph, and closed her eyes. She quickly opened them shortly afterwards because an eerie feeling came over her. She saw that the light was turned on again.

"Since you want to sleep out here, you won't be getting any sleep tonight." He turned on all the lights in the downstairs part of the house. He then turned up the volume on the TVs and turned on the radio.

"What in the hell is wrong with you?" she asked.

"You don't want to sleep in the bed with me. We will both be up all night!" he replied.

Yvette could not believe Joseph's behavior. She sat up on the sofa. Katrina was sound asleep due to the medication. She hadn't heard anything and Jaden stayed at a friend's house that night. Yvette was visibly tired and exhausted. She continued to sit while Joseph went into the kitchen and rummaged through cabinets. He tried to make any extra noise he could possibly make to keep her from sleeping. He was caught, and apparently a switch went off in his head that changed him from the man she thought she loved. His demeanor changed, the look in his eyes changed — everything changed.

He walked over to Yvette and grabbed her by her wrist and asked, "Are you coming to bed or what?"

"Let go of me!" she demanded. "I said I'm sleeping here."

She looked him in his eyes sternly, but all the while her stomach quivered in fear. He had never grabbed her like that. Apparently she won the standoff because Joseph released her wrist and begin to turn everything off. Ultimately, he retreated back into the bedroom, but before he went in and closed the door, he said, "You better figure out what you want to do and where you want to be and you better do it quickly."

Surprisingly, he didn't slam the door to the bedroom. That night, she hardly got any sleep at all but she managed to doze off just before day break. She woke up shortly afterwards to daylight. Joseph seemed to have already got an early start to work. She didn't even hear him leave. After checking to make sure Katrina was okay, she got dressed for work.

When she made it into the office that morning after hardly any sleep, she felt tired and horrible and her co-worker, Mia, couldn't wait to let her know how she looked.

"Dang, girl! You look a mess. What's wrong? This is so not like you," Mia stated.

"Look, I didn't get any sleep last night. Something happened with Katrina at school. I had to go and get her."

She paused before going into any more details. "I'm just tired," she said.

"I can see that," Mia said. "You should have just called off."

"Yeah, I know, but I'm already behind on some reports I really need to get caught up."

"I hear you, girl. If you need any help, let me know."

"Okay, thanks." Mia left Yvette's office to go and take care of some pertinent things in her own office.

CHAPTER 11
FIGHT OR FLIGHT — THE BEGINNING OF THE END

Over the next few days, Joseph's behavior became increasingly more disturbing. Yvette still slept on the sofa and tried to figure out which way to go. She never shared her findings with anyone in her family. She also never confirmed nor denied them with Elisha or Kelsey. She wanted to figure out if she would stay in it or leave. She had one foot out and the other foot was not far behind it. Her marriage was a lie. The man she married no longer existed.

Now that he had been exposed, he had become the man that hid behind another man the whole time. Yvette decided to plan an exit strategy. She had enough. She didn't alert anyone. She wanted to do it on her own. She kept quiet about Joseph's behavior and aggressive personality. So many things weighed in on Yvette — Katrina's suicide attempt, her marriage, and how to start over again. She also thought about the embarrassment and the shame of another failed marriage because she wasn't patient enough to wait. She didn't truly work on herself, she didn't wait for self-healing, neither did she wait for her children to adjust and make sure they were okay. *It was selfish* she thought, *all about Yvette* like Elisha had said.

Later that day, she went to have a drink alone at happy hour at Club Ignite. Why she chose to go there out of all places, she didn't know. Yvette was never the type to normally go out by herself, therefore this was different. It was on her normal route home from work and it was familiar. It was just off the highway. Yvette didn't want to cry about anything anymore, she wanted to drink and relax her mind and hope that the liquor would help her think better. She sat in the back corner to make it difficult for anyone to see her right off. "Can I get you something to drink?" the waitress asked.

"Yes," Yvette said. "A glass of Chardonnay please."

"Will you be getting anything to eat for happy hour?" the waitress asked.

"I'm not sure right now," Yvette replied.

"If you decide to, please do it in the next 30 minutes or so because our happy hour prices changes to regular menu prices."

"Okay, thanks for letting me know."

A few minutes later, the waitress returned with her drink. A couple of sips into her drink, she looked up and was shocked. If there were a back door nearby she would have run out of it, but there wasn't one. She also wished there was a button that would open up a trap door where she could fall through the floor and disappear. There wasn't such a thing. She was stuck in that spot and tried hard to make herself look as inconspicuous as possible. The first chance she gets, she would make a break for the door. It was too late. She looked up and her eyes met his. He looked surprised to see her there after all this time. *Oh my God,* Yvette said to herself with her stomach in knots. *Why did I have to come here today, better yet, why did I have to come here at all?* He began to make his way over to where Yvette sat.

"Long time," he said in a deep and sexy undertone that slowly snapped her out of her "woe is me" trance for a moment. The smell of his cologne took her back. Not much had changed about him. He had the same swagger, the same charming attitude, and same fuckboy looks.

"Hey, Dalvin, what's up?" she asked.

"Last I heard, you got married. How's that going?" he asked.

"It's going," Yvette replied.

"I see you are drinking Chardonnay. I guess it's going down tonight for the husband, huh?" he smirked.

Yvette didn't respond. She didn't know why she chose Chardonnay out of all the drinks she could have ordered. Nothing sexual was going on in her home tonight at all.

"I only wanted to stop by and speak. You know Club Ambiance is open again. I'm back promoting there now. You and your girls should come through. Bring your husband, too," he said slyly and walked away.

Same cocky, arrogant ass, Dalvin. Yvette never had closure with him and as bad as she felt he hurt her, his presence still made her body tingle. She sipped on the remainder of her drink and allowed her mind to go back. It retraced the days of burning up the highway at any chance just to feel his touch, his kiss, and his hands, all over her body. She remembered the way he took control in the bedroom and the feel of his body thrusting back and forth aggressively against hers. Yep, the tie was not completely broken. She decided it was time for her to go home.

Yvette pulled into the driveway. The car belonging to Joseph, Steven, or whatever name he used, was already there. Yvette took a deep breath. She wished for a do-over. She wanted to get back to when it was only her, Katrina, and Jaden. She took a long look at the enormous house they lived in and the gorgeous neighborhood. Now, it all meant absolutely nothing. She entered the house, and as usual, threw her keys in the bowl on the table in the foyer. She anticipated what would come but never expected what would happen next. She went into the master bedroom where Joseph watched TV. She was still angry about everything that transpired. She grabbed a few items of clothing with the intentions of showering upstairs and sleeping on the sofa again. Thankfully, Jaden's shower had been fixed.

"So, you're not going to speak?" Joseph asked.

"It depends on who I'm speaking to," Yvette said smartly. "I'm still trying to figure out who I married." She headed upstairs. Katrina and Jaden were in their rooms. They had no idea what went on between their mother and step-father. They knew nothing about Joseph really being Steven.

"Mom, why are you taking a shower up here?" Jaden asked.

"Joseph is doing something in our bathroom. Besides, I haven't seen you guys in a minute."

"I know, this house is so big," Katrina stated. "We could literally go for days and not cross paths."

"I don't even go towards your room if you're not home. I barely want to go in there when you are there, ever since the shower incident. I know he apologized, but I rather stay out of his way, you know," Jaden said.

This made Yvette angry and sad at the same time. Her children were her world and should never have been made to feel uncomfortable in a house that they lived in. She showered, talked with them for a couple of hours, then went downstairs. She took her work clothes into the bedroom where Joseph was still awake. He was watching TV. Yvette put her clothing into the hamper in the bathroom, came out and grabbed a pillow from the bed. She went into the hallway and retrieved extra bedding and laid down on the sofa. A few minutes later, Joseph came into the room.

"Is this how it's going to be?" he asked.

Yvette became aggressive. "Joseph, Steven, whoever you are, you lied to me this whole time. Everything is bullshit, this marriage, this house, everything."

"What do you want to do, huh?" he asked angrily. "You want to be with that mother fucker you were with at happy hour earlier? Yeah, my boy saw you smiling up in his face. Yet you get here and have a fucking frown on your face."

"What do I need to smile at you for? Your personality has changed. You're not the man I married. I don't want to be here anymore. I don't want this marriage."

Joseph looked like someone had gut punched him. He looked at Yvette as though a veil was lifted from his face and he became who he tried to hide.

"There's only one way out of this he said with a look of sheer evil in his eyes and walked away."

"So, you're fucking threatening me now?" Yvette yelled. "You're threatening me? Okay, since you want to threaten me, let me get the police involved."

Joseph let out a sinister laugh, went back into the bedroom and closed the door. Yvette didn't know how to take the statement he made, nevertheless she called the police and made them aware of Joseph's threat. They asked her if he had physically harmed her? Since he had not, she was informed they would take her statement, but there was nothing they could do in that moment. Yvette hung up the phone. She sat up on the sofa with her nerves and mind all over the place. She wanted to call someone, but she was still determined to keep things to herself. *I got myself in this, I'm going to get myself out.* She grabbed a knife from the knife block in the kitchen and placed it under her pillow. There was no more trust, as far as she was concerned. Marrying him was the second biggest mistake of her life. It took some hours after that, but Yvette managed to fall asleep for five minutes and she felt a presence standing over her in the dark. It was Joseph.

"No wife of mine will continue to sleep on the couch!" Yvette awakened startled like before. She reached for the knife that she had placed under her pillow and brandished it at Joseph. She jumped to her feet to stand at his level. She looked in his eyes. Yvette thought he would feel threatened and leave her alone. She was wrong.

"Oh, you are going to stab me? Well, stab me then!" he shouted and moved closer to her. He then took out his phone and dialed 911. "Since you want to call the police, let me call them and let them know that you pulled a knife on me."

In an instant, he tried to wrestle the knife from her hand. Yvette never wanted to stab him, she only wanted to scare him. The tussle over the knife was on. His phone dropped with a 911 operator on the other end. "911 what is your emergency?" the operator repeated. The operator heard yelling and a struggle. Joseph managed to get the knife out of Yvette's hands. She was shocked and afraid of what he would do now that he had the knife. She could only think about her children. *What if he kills me and then goes upstairs and kills the children?* she thought. At that moment, she developed the strength of what seemed like 10 men. It became the fight of her life. She pushed and grabbed at Joseph until she was able to get the knife back in her possession. In the process, she grabbed the knife by the blade and sliced open the palm of her hand and the tip of her index finger. Because of her adrenaline rush, she never felt a thing. Joseph tried to grab her. Yvette sliced at the hand that reached for her and sliced Joseph across his chest. The second cut seemed to stun Joseph. He stopped and looked at Yvette in disbelief.

"Leave me alone, Joseph!" she cried. She couldn't believe what had happened. Joseph was bleeding. Blood dripped from his hand. He raised his shirt up to see a superficial wound to his chest. The knife sliced completely through his shirt. The wound to his hand was more severe. It finally clicked when she felt moisture in her hand that she had been injured as well. Yvette began to sob uncontrollably. Joseph noticed his phone was on the floor. He picked it up but there was no one on the other end.

"Look, I called 911. They're probably going to come here anyway. We need to figure out what we're going to tell them or we both are going to probably end up in jail." Joseph also knew he had a previous situation that involved the police. He did not want them to get involved.

"Why didn't you leave me alone?" she cried. "Look we need to make them feel like everything is good. We need to get cleaned up. I love you, Yvette. I didn't want this. We got to stick together in this."

Yvette, like most ordinary people, had a fear of going to jail. If what he was saying is true she was willing to do whatever was necessary. They wiped up the blood, changed clothes, washed and bandaged their wounds to the best of their ability in the few minutes they figured they had. Yvette went into her walk-in closet and pulled down all of her clothing that were on hangers. She began to pack her things. She cried and sobbed severely. There was a loud banging at the front door. Joseph came into the closet and said, "The police are at the door. You have to answer. Stop crying. I'm going to stay in the room. Tell them we had an argument but all is well now."

The banging intensified. Yvette composed herself the best she could and went to the door.

"Who is it?" she asked.

"It's Dallas PD. Ma'am open the door."

The 911 call was traced to their home. The operator reported hearing a woman yelling and screaming. Yvette opened the door, but balled up her injured hand and tried her best to keep it from their view. Two officers were at the door. One male and one female.

"Can I help you?" she asked.

"Ma'am, we received a 911 call about a possible domestic situation going on here. Can we come in?"

With the door slightly ajar, Yvette said, "We had a minor argument, but all is well now."

"Can we come in?" the officer asked once more. Yvette hesitated at first but then allowed the officers to come in. When she opened the door completely, she saw that the corner lot where their house sat was lit up like a Christmas tree. Not only were there two officers inside the house, but four cars were outside with their lights flashing. Two other officers were on the lawn and two sat in their cars.

"Where's your husband?" the male officer asked.

"He's in the shower."

"Go get him," the female officer demanded. She went into the room to find Joseph still trying to bandage his hand. The blood kept soaking through.

"The officers want to see you," she told him.

"Okay, just tell them I will be out in a minute."

Yvette went back out to tell the officers what Joseph said. Her heart was beating fast. After a couple of minutes, Joseph came out.

"Hi, officers. Can I help you?" he asked.

We got a 911 call from this location that sounded like a domestic situation. Is every thing okay?" The female officer took charge.

"Yes, officer. We had a little disagreement. All is well."

Without warning, blood poured from Joseph's injured hand. It saturated the makeshift bandage and dripped onto the floor in front of the officers. They noticed it and became alarmed.

"What happened to your hand, sir?" the male officer questioned.

"There was a broken glass in my dish water earlier I didn't know about. When I reached in, it sliced my hand." Joseph was quick with his thoughts like any good liar.

"Is that true, ma'am?" he asked.

"Yes," Yvette answered.

Sensing something wasn't right, the female officer asked to speak with Yvette outside. Joseph stayed inside with the other officer. Yvette stood on the porch wearing a T-shirt and a pair of leggings. Her hair was pulled back in a ponytail and she was barefoot. Although it was midnight, she knew all the neighbors were looking out of their windows. And those who weren't, would find out from the others tomorrow. She was sure of that. She was interrogated for half an hour.

"What happened here tonight?" The female officer asked.

"We got into an argument. You know how that is," she said nervously.

"How did his hand get cut, again?"

Yvette repeated the same story Joseph did, but the officer wasn't buying it at all.

"Are you afraid to be here tonight? Are you afraid of him?"

Yvette looked at the officer and said, "No, I'm okay." She gave a fake smile.

"You know after they could not get an answer from the 911 call, we traced it to your address. The operator said she heard a female screaming."

"Yeah, I yelled at him because I was angry."

Still not convinced, the officer told Yvette to stay there while she went inside to speak with the other officer. They both came out and left Joseph inside. They then walked to their cars and had a discussion with the rest of the officers. The original two officers walked back to the house.

"Ma'am, we don't know what went on here tonight but we're going to ask that one of you spend the night elsewhere, just for tonight," the female officer stated.

"My children are asleep upstairs," Yvette said.

"We don't want you to wake them."

The officers asked Joseph to pack a bag and spend the night somewhere else. Joseph did so and got into his car, but not before giving Yvette a concerned look.

"Get that hand looked at," the male officer told him and he left as instructed.

"Call us if he returns tonight because if he does, he will be arrested."

The officers got into their cars and left. When Yvette went back inside, she looked up and saw Katrina and Jaden. They looked down from the balcony that overlooked the foyer. They were awakened by the sound of the officers banging on the door. Yvette spent the next hour explaining everything to them in the game room. Jaden was upset that he was not awake to protect his mom. He punched a hole in the wall. After looking at his bruised knuckles, she apologized profusely for putting her wants and desires before them. She told them they would move and that they should begin to pack later that day. She went downstairs to check all the doors and set the house alarm. By the time everything was over, it was 4 am and she had to be at work at 9 am. She couldn't afford to call off.

Yvette managed to get two hours of sleep before she forced herself out of bed to get ready for work. She was exhausted and looked every bit of it. No amount of makeup could cover it up and make up for the lack of sleep. She tried as best as she could in spite of it all. She threw on a pair of gray slacks with a black and white pin-striped shirt and black pumps. She flat-ironed her long black tresses down her back. Yvette's hand began to throb. It finally set in that her hand had been severely sliced open when she grabbed the blade of the knife in an effort to save her life and possibly her children's life.

She did not want anyone to know the depth of her marital problems. Her mind was made up to continue to keep everything to herself. She wanted to get out of that house as soon as possible. First she needed to attend to her hand. She went into the bathroom and retrieved a first-aid kit. She cleaned and wrapped her hand. She arrived at work with her hand bandaged and visibly exhausted for the second time. She ran into Mia in the hallway before she could get into her office. She saw Yvette's hand was wrapped and that she looked like she hadn't slept in days.

Mia said, "Just tell me where we need to hide the body."

"What?" Yvette replied. She was confused.

"I'm not going to ask any questions ... just tell me where we need to hide the body. What happened to your hand?" Mia asked.

"Oh, I cut it on a broken glass in the sink while I washed dishes."

"Really?" Mia peered at her suspiciously. She knew she was lying.

"Yes," she responded and tried to walk to her office. She didn't want to deal with this, at least not now.

"Look, like I told you. I'm here if you need me."

"Yes, I know," Yvette said.

That day she replayed the night's events over and over in her head. She saw all of the red flags leading up to it. She was mentally drained but still needed to focus on work. She no longer felt safe in her home but she didn't want to alert anyone concerning what transpired until it was done.

A couple of days went by and Yvette and the children finished packing. Yvette had signed a lease on an apartment but it wouldn't be ready for two weeks. She would continue to reside in the house with Joseph until then. Yvette moved upstairs with the children to keep distance between her and him. The house was big enough for them to never cross paths unless they both utilizing the kitchen at the same time. Yvette made sure that didn't happen by constantly eating out. With each passing day, the house looked more empty. A house that was once decorated beautifully was now practically an empty shell, filled with moving boxes. It was so empty now that it echoed whenever someone talked.

Seeing his world and his marriage falling apart due to his lies and anger issues made Joseph agitated . He could not stand the fact she was leaving him and there was nothing he could do about it. He tried countless times to pick fights and argue with her about petty things, like the possibility of her taking his items along with hers as she packed. He also wanted gifts back that he had bought for her and so on.

One time Joseph was petty enough to ask Yvette for an Apple tablet he had purchased for her. She replied, "If you give me all the pussy back that I gave you, then you can have it. Until then, leave me the fuck alone. Let's just get through this and be done with this sham of a marriage."

One day, she went into the front yard to sit by herself, in order to get away from his antics and he followed her and antagonized her. Yvette got tired of it and she told him to leave her alone and to stop acting like a little boy. This angered him. A loud argument ensued. One of the neighbors called the cops. When the officers pulled up, Joseph and Yvette was so engaged in their argument they didn't even notice.

"Hey! What's going on? What's the problem?" the officer asked. To her surprise, one of the officers was with the group that came out the night of the previous incident.

"There's no problem, officer," Joseph responded. "We're just having a disagreement."

The officer turned to Yvette. "Ma'am what's going on?"

"I have decided to move out of the house. I'm waiting for my apartment to be ready. I reside in the upper portion of the home away from him and I just want to be left alone until I leave and he won't quit harassing me. I just want to move peacefully," Yvette replied.

"Sir, if the home is big enough for the two of you to split up and remain out of each other's way until then, I suggest you do that and leave her alone. Do not go upstairs until she has moved out. If we have to come back to this residence again for someone disturbing the peace, one of you will be arrested. Do the two of you understand?"

"Yes," they both replied.

The officers got into their patrol car and drove away. Yvette was embarrassed to have the police at her home for the second time in a matter of days. Little did she know that would not be the last time. With the sporadic behavior that Joseph or Steven exhibited, she was afraid now and did not know what to expect from one day to the next. She still had a little over a week before her apartment would be ready for move-in. She needed something that would scare him more than a knife would and she knew just who to call, Mitchell.

Although he was extremely disappointed that Yvette married someone else, Mitchell still loved and cared about her tremendously. He resided in the same location so she called him and met him at his home later that evening. She rang the doorbell and Mitchell opened the door and smiled from ear-to-ear. Her presence made him light up.

"Come on in," he urged. "Give me a hug." The two embraced and Mitchell hugged her tightly as if he didn't want to let go. Yvette kissed him on the cheek. "Have a seat," Mitchell said. "To what do I owe the pleasure? I didn't think I would ever see you again being that you went off and got married and all."

"Yeah, I didn't think I would be sitting here in your living room again, either," she replied. "What's up?" he inquired.

"Remember when you loaned me your gun a couple of years ago? I need to borrow it again. Please don't ask me any questions."

"I have to, being as though you're asking for a gun that's registered to me."

"My marriage isn't working out. I'm trying to relocate. We have had a couple of incidents and I don't feel safe. It will be just until I move, please."

Mitchell was a fool for Yvette's beauty. He cared for her and couldn't ever say no to her. Without any more questions he went upstairs to retrieve the gun he had let her hold before.

"You remember how to use this right?" he asked.

"Yes, I do," she responded.

He handed her the box containing a 9 mm Ruger.

He looked at her and said, "Let me see your foot."

"What? Why?" Yvette asked.

"Let me see your foot," he repeated once more.

She held up her foot and Mitchell grabbed it in his hand. Yvette always kept her feet and nails nicely done. She had on a pair of rhinestone sandals that exposed her toes that were painted in a bright pink which reflected nicely off her dark skin.

He held her foot in his hand and said, "You are much too beautiful and way too valuable for these two to end up with a tag on them, so please be careful."

That thought resonated deeply with Yvette. They gave each other a hug and said their goodbyes.

CHAPTER 12
WHEN THE SMOKE CLEARS

O ver the course of the next few days, Yvette continued to pack. Her and the children stayed away as much as possible and only came home to sleep and pack for the most part. They stayed out of Joseph's way and out of his sight. There was three days left to go, and the two had managed to reside in the house. One day while at work, Yvette received a call from a strange number. Being curious, she answered it, although as a rule she didn't answer unknown numbers.

"Hello," she answered.

"I need to see you and I'm not taking no for an answer. I'd rather a slow yes than a fast no," the voice on the other end said. There was only one person who ever said that to her, Geo! "Geo, how did you get my number?" Yvette asked.

"I've always had eyes on you, Yvette. And those children. Just because we're not together anymore doesn't mean that I wasn't watching over you and watching out for you. You and those two children are always on my mind and in my heart. Can we please meet and talk?" It had been a minute since she saw him. He used to be her everything.

"Let's just meet up and have a few drinks or some dinner or both," he said.

She hesitated for a minute but she did agree to meet with him. She could most certainly use a goon like Geo and his crew in her corner right now. After work, the two met up at a local restaurant. It was a popular Cajun food spot that had great food and strong drinks. The weather was a little cooler. Yvette wore a pair of stiletto knee high boots, a burgundy sweater, and black form-fitting skinny jeans, and she had loose curls in her Peruvian 18 inch weave, flowing down her back. She waited in front of the restaurant by the hostess stand for Geo to arrive. As she looked over the restaurant watching everyone eat, she heard a voice say, "I see you got your get ones on tonight."

She turned around and her heart practically stopped. There he stood, gold teeth and all, blinging, fresh haircut, smelling delicious, and looking tantalizing wearing a fresh pair of Forces, True Religion jeans and matching T-shirt. Shades adorned his face as usual along with a neatly trimmed goatee, fresh from the barbershop. It was almost like the night of their first date.

"Give me a hug," he said. "I'm not going to bite you." Yvette walked over and gave him a hug. "You feel so good in my arms," he whispered in her ear. Yvette panties immediately got wet. The two sat down and had dinner laughed, talked, and reminisced. "Yvette, you know I loved you so much, it really hurt me when you didn't want to be with me anymore. It took me a minute to get over you. I went back home and stayed low for a minute. My brothers and my partners teased me and called me pussy whipped. They said you must have voodooed me and all that shit. I still have love for you but I respect where you're at. I just had to see you and let you know. I was a man in love who did some stupid shit I'm not proud of. And I wanted to apologize and let you know face to face that I would never do anything to hurt you or those children." Yvette looked into his eyes and saw the sincerity. He meant every word he spoke. "So how's married life? You know I heard about it," he smiled.

"Not the best. Probably will get divorced soon. I'm moving out."

Geo wasn't the type to ask questions or pry. He only said I'm here if you need me. The two finished their meal and drinks, then said their goodbyes after more conversation.

It was near midnight when she arrived at the house that was no longer a home to her. Katrina was asleep in her room and Jaden spent the night at his best friend's house at Yvette's urging. She assured him that she would be okay. Once she peeked in on Katrina, she went into the room that was once her home office, but now had boxes everywhere. She put a futon mattress on the floor for sleeping since all the beds were dismantled and ready to move.

Yvette could hear the TV on downstairs in the bedroom that she and Joseph one shared. She was so ready to go. She felt great about seeing Geo again and putting the past behind them. Not to mention the drinks were great. Yvette got undressed. She removed her sweater and then her pants. Joseph burst into the room.

"So you are going to tramp around now that you're leaving and come in and out of the house when you're ready like I don't exist!" he shouted. She was startled and stood there in her bra and panties.

Finally she said, "You're not supposed to be up here. The police told you to stay downstairs, Joseph. There's no reason for you to be up here."

"This is my house! No one is going to tell me where I can and cannot go. I pay the mortgage!"

"We pay the mortgage. You don't pay it by yourself!" Yvette said.

"Just get out Joseph. I don't have any clothes on."

"I've seen you in your bra and panties before. You're still my wife!" Joseph paused and stared at Yvette's underwear for a minute.

"Why is your underwear inside out?" he asked.

"What?" Yvette said and looked down. Apparently in her haste to get to work she had put her panties on, on the wrong side. It's an easy mistake being that they were so thin.

"You are fucking somebody," he yelled! "You fucking whore, you couldn't wait 'till you were out of the house, that's why you have been coming in so late. That's why it's so easy for you to leave me!"

"I haven't been fucking anyone!" Yvette yelled.

"You're a lying bitch!" Joseph yelled once more.

"Okay, get out before I call the police," Yvette tried to push Joseph out of the door. She had him halfway out of the door when Joseph gave her one big push that sent her flying backwards onto the floor. She landed on her back on the futon. Joseph landed on top of her and started to strangle her.

Katrina was awakened by the commotion and saw Joseph trying to choke the life out of her mom as Yvette clawed at his face. Katrina jumped on his back and yelled, "Get off my mom! Get off my mom!"

Yvette thought she would pass out from Joseph's grip around her neck, but she remembered she had Mitchell's gun hidden underneath the futon. She didn't want to kill him or hurt him, but she had to find a way to let him know she meant business. The gun was intended to keep him away from her and the children. In this moment it was about her life. She reached underneath the side of the futon with the last bit of energy and breath she had as Joseph continued to choke her. She grabbed the gun which was ready to be fired and shot two rounds into the ceiling of the house as warning shots. Joseph realized she had a gun and quickly jumped up. Katrina helped her mom get to her feet.

Yvette pointed the gun at him and said, "I asked you to leave me alone didn't I? And you just couldn't! Katrina hand me my phone." Katrina did as her mom instructed. Yvette dialed 911.

"911 what's your emergency?" the operator asked.

"Can you please send someone to 1835 Poppyseed Trail. My husband just tried to choke me to death."

While she was on the phone and distracted, Joseph took off and ran down the stairs. Yvette ran out after him, gun in hand, but before she could get down the stairs she heard Katrina scream, "Mom, no!"

The sound of Katrina's voice stopped her dead in her tracks. She turned and looked at her daughter and cried while she grabbed and hugged her. Yvette put away the gun but before she could walk out of the door and head down the stairs, the police were on their way up the stairs.

"Ma'am, I'm going to need you to come with us please," the officer said.

"But why? I'm the one who called you! That bastard was choking the life out of me!" Yvette yelled. "Ask my daughter, she's a witness."

"Ma'am is the weapon still in your possession?"

"I put it back under the mattress," she answered.

"Step outside of the room completely," the officer demanded. Yvette did as she was told. "Turn around and put your hands behind your back."

"Why? Why, officer, am I being arrested when I'm the victim here? I'm the one who called."

"Ma'am you're under arrest for unlawfully firing a weapon inside of residence."

"He would have choked me to death had I not shot it! Are you serious?"

"Ma'am, please don't make this any more difficult than it has to be."

"Mom what should I do?" Katrina asked with tears in her eyes.

"Don't do anything and don't say anything to anyone. I will figure it out. Take care of your brother. I will call you shortly." Katrina stood there looking helpless. "I love you. Don't worry, okay?

Yvette held back tears and tried to stay strong in order for Katrina to be strong. On her way downstairs she could hear Joseph, lying to the police officer. As Yvette was put in the back of the squad car she and Joseph locked eyes for what she knew would be the last time. Or so she prayed. Yvette was booked into the county jail on a weapon possession charge and unlawfully discharge of a firearm inside of a residence. Her biggest fear had been brought to reality. She was in jail. Yvette did not know what to do. She was fingerprinted and her mugshot was taken. She was also tested for TB before they placed her in a holding cell with some other females. The jail cell was as cold as a freezer. Yvette only had on a sundress and flip flops when she was arrested. It was so cold she thought she would pass out from hypothermia. She sat Indian style on the bench and used the length of her dress to cover her legs and tucked her arms inside the dress in an effort to get as warm as possible, but it didn't work much at all.

Although she was afraid, she didn't want it to show on her face. Some of the ladies got bonded out but Yvette didn't know what to do. Seeing the confusion on Yvette's face, one of the women asked, "Do you know what your bond is? If you know what your bond is, you can call your family and have them get you a bondsman to get you out."

Yvette said, "Thanks."

"Girl, I'm in here for a DUI. I switched places with my drunk-ass boyfriend so he wouldn't get pulled over and we got pulled over anyway because I was almost as drunk as him," the woman said. "I told his crazy ass we should have gotten a hotel and sobered up until we could make it home. Well, I'm sober as hell now. This cold ass cell made sure of that! I should be getting out soon though, they already have my bond and found me a bondsman. Just go ask the guard if they have set bond for you, yet," she urged.

Yvette did as instructed, and found out her bond was set at $10,000 and 10% would have to be paid up front for her to be released. There was a phone on the wall as well as a list of bail bond companies. Yvette didn't want to call any of her family members. They didn't have $1,000 sitting around like that but she did. The problem was, it was in her bank account and the police had taken her things. She swallowed her pride and called the one person she didn't want to call but who would know exactly how to help her. Elisha. She picked up the phone and dialed her number.

"You have a call from Dallas County Jail from Yvette," the operator stated when Elisha answered.

"Bitch! I know you lying!" Elisha shouted. "Yes, I will accept the charges. Hello, Yvette?"

"Yeah," Yvette replied.

"Bitch, I know you fucking lying! What in the hell?" Elisha laughed hysterically. "What are you doing in jail?"

"Joseph, or should I say Stephen and I got into it. He choked me and I fired a gun to get him off me."

"Wait, choked, gun? What the hell?" she responded.

"Elisha, I can talk to you later about it. I just want to get out of here. I feel like the walls are closing in on me. I have a list of bail bonds people here. Can you call them, please? My bond is set at $10,000. I need $1,000 to get out.

"Bitch, where am I going to get it from! Just sit it out and see the judge Monday and keep your cash. Hell, when I was arrested on the weekend, I just got comfortable, ate my little bag lunch, made me some friends and chilled."

"Elisha, I'm serious. I can't stay in here much longer. I'm freaking out on the inside and I don't know how much longer I can hold on."

"Okay okay," she laughed. "Let me make a few phone calls to get your bougie ass out."

Yvette hung up the phone. Yvette sat and waited for what seemed like an eternity. Everyone was seemingly getting called to get bonded out but her. She trusted that Elisha would help her out because she was completely clueless and didn't want to worry or scare her mom. Another hour went by and an officer came in. It was time to go into general population for those who had not bonded out yet. Yvette's heart sank, and she began to tremble uncontrollably. Everyone was lead into individual rooms, made to strip off their street clothes, and was searched and probed. Yvette was made to squat and cough just as she saw in the movies.

She was treated like a common criminal, given jail house issued attire, and bedding. The walk to general population was a long one. As they trekked down the hall, the male inmates were made to face the wall while they passed by. Yvette could not take it anymore. She crumbled to the floor and sobbed uncontrollably to the point she hyperventilated.

"Get up inmate," the officer commanded. Yvette couldn't stand. She was broken. She thought about was her children and her life. How did it get to this place? The escorting officer bent down and whispered something in her ear that would make her straighten up for the duration of her stay.

"Look, I know you have children," the officer started.

"If you continue to cry in this manner, they will think that you are suicidal and treat you as a danger to yourself, throw you into an empty cell, naked with nothing but a suicide blanket, which will make your stay here much longer."

Yvette got up instantly. Staying longer was definitely not an option. She wiped her tears and put on the bravest face she possibly could. Once inside the general population, women everywhere seemed to be comfortable. Jail was something Yvette could never get used to. She looked around and spotted the one thing that cheered her up a little, a phone. She was given her cell number and told to go make her bed. As she entered, she saw someone was already asleep in one of the beds. Once she entered the doors, they closed automatically behind her, and the sound was one she would never forget as long as she lived. She quickly made her bed then tapped on the window of the door and asked if she could use the phone. Once the officer verified that her bed was made, she allowed her to make a phone call. She called Elisha again.

"Hey, girl what's going on? Have y'all gotten someone? They got me in the back now," Yvette whispered.

Elisha laughed, "They got a bitch in jail jail," she teased. "You are going to be okay."

"Elisha, this isn't funny!"

"Calm down and get your lil bag lunch. We are working on it. We got a bail bondsman and you should be getting out soon."

"We who?" Yvette asked. "I made a few phone calls. I figured you had been given these bastards free pussy, the least they could do is help you out and one came through so sit tight," Elisha said.

"Why did you tell anyone?" Yvette shouted. "It was none of their business."

"It wasn't mine either, but you called me. And your pussy was their business at one point so why not capitalize on it? That's what's wrong with your ass, scared to be vulnerable when it comes down to it. I didn't have it, and my stripper skills aren't what they used to be."

"Who is it?" Yvette asked.

"You will see," Elisha said. "Now sit down, relax get your lunch like I said, and stay cool. The bond has been paid you'll be out soon."

"Thank you, Elisha. I know we have had our times but I really appreciate you."

"It's all good. Don't drop the soap bitch," she said and laughed hysterically. Yvette managed to laugh a little then hung up the phone.

The waiting game began. Although she was exhausted, she did not sleep one wink since her arrest. She watched a couple of other girls get bonded out who were in the holding cell with her. She started to get nervous again. It was getting late. *I can't sleep here I can't. I'm going to lose my mind if I stay in here any longer.* Suicidal thoughts begin to cloud her mind.

I can't stay here. I would rather die. Yvette also wondered if Elisha had contacted anyone at all. *I need to go ahead and call my mom,* she thought. The chaos in her head ensued and she walked towards the phone to call her mom. Before she could make it to her destination, she heard her name being called. "Inmate Yvette Jennings." She felt what seemed like a cool rush of water flow over her body. She turned around and walked over to the officer who had called her name.

"Yes ma'am?" Yvette answered.

"Your bond has been made. Gather your bedding and come with me."

Yvette was ecstatic. She didn't show it on her face, but her insides danced with relief. Once outside of general population, Yvette was led to a room where she received her street clothing and told to get dressed. It was still a waiting game after that, but it was one that she didn't mind playing now. She felt human and normal again. After about an hour, she was called to a window to retrieve her personal belongings such as purse and cell phone. There she was also given the contingencies of her bond. She was then escorted out of a door into a waiting area.

Her benefactor stood smiling and waiting for her. She ran into his arms like a little girl running into her father's arms. Not only because it was him but also because she was glad to be free.

"Elisha told me to tell you the children are at Kelsey's house for the night and they also took old boy to jail after getting a statement from your daughter. He's not allowed back in the house until you all have completely moved your things," he said. She also enlisted the help of one of your co-workers along with herself to help with the move. I think she said some chick named Mia."

"Oh, my God. Now everybody knows my business," Yvette said with embarrassment.

"Hey, you're out and you're good. That's all that matters. I figured I'd get you a hotel room for the night so you can rest," he stated.

"Awwww, thanks. That's sweet of you."

Once at the hotel, Yvette showered for at least an hour. She wanted to get as much of the feel of jail off of her as possible. Since she had nothing but the clothes she wore when she got arrested, she wrapped herself in a huge white robe that hung inside the hotel's closet. She then laid across the bed and exhaled deeply.

"Okay, I'm going to let you get some rest. Call me in the morning when you get up. I will come back and get you and take you to Kelsey's house to see your children."

"Why are you leaving? Please stay."

"I have some things I have to get done," he responded. He took one look at Yvette's disappointed face and decided to stay. He didn't get undressed. He simply took off his shoes and climbed in bed. He sat upright with his back against the headboard and they began to watch TV. Yvette did not sleep the entire 16 hours she was incarcerated. She was extremely tired, mentally and physically. She laid her head on his lap and instantly fell asleep. He watched her sleep and stroked her face. He couldn't deny it, he really cared for her. Day turned into night, then into day again. Yvette awoke to him staring down at her as he flipped channels on the TV. He had not moved from that spot. He allowed her to sleep.

"You've been awake all this time," she asked.

"No," he laughed. "I nodded off here and there."

"Why didn't you move me so you can lay down?"

"You were sleeping so peacefully and you were tired. But I do have to go to the bathroom now," he laughed.

Yvette raised up and allowed him to go to the bathroom to relieve himself. He stood up and stretched to get the blood back flowing through his body. Yvette watched him walk away. She checked out his shoulders and his back and began to reminisced. When he returned, she was just staring at him.

"Why are you looking at me like that?" he asked.

"Kiss me," she said.

"Yvette, I know you're vulnerable right now. I don't want you to do anything you will regret."

"I won't. I need this. I need to feel the things I used to feel just for a moment with no strings. I just need this."

He saw the look of desperation in her eyes and the need to feel released and he obliged. He leaned down and kissed her softly on her lips. Yvette's body settled like feet in sinking sand. He laid her back on the bed and opened the robe she wore and exposed her naked body. Her dark tone skin against the pure white robe looked like heaven and hell at the same time. And if her body was hell he was about to burst through heaven and shake hands with the devil face first. It had been awhile since he had touched her. He took his time gently kissing and caressing her gently. Yvette moaned at every touch. Her body throbbed and waited to receive him. And then it happened, pure injection. Like the song from the Boyz II Men, the scene played out in that manner. Lots of uhhhhs and ahhhhs filled the room. She felt his vigorous thrusting and the feel of his shaft deep inside of her. She squeezed him tight and ran her hands across his broad shoulders and kissed his neck. His thrusts became more intense as the climax started to build between the both of them. He had her reaching for things that did not exist. Yvette didn't want anything to come of this but it was what she needed in the moment. So long to the 50-yard Dash, hello, Marathon Man. She missed him desperately and needed him as much.

Once it was all said and done, they laid there and enjoyed one another's company as they talked about old times. Then the reality of it all hit. It was time to get her life back on track. She had to put away her desires and step away to take some time out to work on herself and to be there for her children. She would never let anything or any one possess her thoughts in any manner whatsoever. She made up her mind in that moment to gain control of herself and eliminate things that would destroy her, once and for all. It was time to recognize her worth. Tumultuous apogee!

www.ingramcontent.com/pod-product-compliance
Lightning Source LLC
Chambersburg PA
CBHW030247030726
47493CB00023B/1311